Winthrop Sargent, Joseph Stansbury, Jonathan Odell

The Loyal Verses of Joseph Stansbury

and Doctor Jonathan Odell relating to the American Revolution

Winthrop Sargent, Joseph Stansbury, Jonathan Odell

The Loyal Verses of Joseph Stansbury
and Doctor Jonathan Odell relating to the American Revolution

ISBN/EAN: 9783337237790

Printed in Europe, USA, Canada, Australia, Japan

Cover: Foto ©Andreas Hilbeck / pixelio.de

More available books at **www.hansebooks.com**

Munsell's

Historical Series.

No. VI.

THE

𝕷𝖔𝖞𝖆𝖑 𝖁𝖊𝖗𝖘𝖊𝖘

OF

JOSEPH STANSBURY

AND

Doctor JONATHAN ODELL;

RELATING TO THE

AMERICAN REVOLUTION.

———

NOW FIRST EDITED

By WINTHROP SARGENT.

———

ALBANY:
J. MUNSELL, 78 STATE STREET.
1860.

Aux Lecteurs.

Amys lecteurs, qui ce liure lisez,
Despouillez vous de toute affection;
Et le lisant ne vous scandalisez.
Il ne contient mal ne infection.
Vray est qu'icy peu de perfection
Vous apprendrez ———   Rabelais.

PREFACE.

THE collection and prefervation of the ancient Songs of a Nation has long been esteemed a worthy occupation. In other lands than this, thefe refearches, it is true, go back to days of chivalry and are rewarded by the acquifition of

> What refounds,
> In fable or romance, of Uther's fon
> Begirt with Britifh or Armoric knights.

In our own country, the range of inquiry is more limited. We have no fuch legendary treafures to draw upon. The invention of printing—the ufe of gunpowder—the extenfion of navigation—all the difcoveries that moulded the form and character of modern times, and feparate us from paft ages, preceded the European fettlements in America, and fhut out from our foil the

B   growth

growth of any fchool of fiction akin to thofe that had flourifhed on the other continent. The *Golden Legends* of the monks; the romances of knight-errantry; the fatirical *Sirventes* of the troubadours—found no fucceffors here. And while various circumftances hindered the new comers from bequeathing to this the local literatures of their own lands, other caufes operated with equal force to prevent the early developement of anything like a national department of our own. Such tales and legends of thofe days as have come down to us are now as valuable for their rarity as for their nature. Obfcure and remote, the Colonies for a long while fcarcely claimed among themfelves, and certainly did not obtain from Europe, the flighteft confideration on the fcore of mental excellence or cultivation. So effentially were they in the fhade, that it is told as a probable, if not a true ftory, that Cromwell would fain have fought refuge here, as in an impenetrable covert, from the wrath of the Court; and if his efcape from the Thames was obftructed by the officers of Charles, it was in all likelihood becaufe they conceived him about to fly into regions where it would be difficult to purfue and impoffible to detect him. And many years later, when pious men from Virginia befought official favour in England to their fcheme of eftablifhing a College in that Colony, fo flight was the efteem in which American intelligence was held that the Attorney-
General

General ftared in utter amazement at the propofition. "Why, what in Heaven's name," he exclaimed, "do "you want with a College in Virginia?" "To im- "prove the minds and the fouls of the youth of the "province," was the humble reply. "Souls!" cried the law-dignitary, aghaft at fuch prefumption—"*Souls!* "*D— your fouls! make tobacco!*"

Thus it happens that we find very little of local fiction in any of its ordinary forms, among our ancient American literature. The Revolutionary War, how- ever, which gave this country a feat in the circle of empires, was fucceeded by an unlooked for and won- derful profperity, that foon raifed it to greatnefs. And as this conteft—the moft important epoch in our na- tional hiftory—was not at all deficient in thofe political verfes that naturally find their feat upon the lips of men engaged in a long and impaffioned ftrife, it does not ill become us, who today enjoy the fruit of the arduous toils of the founders of our State, to regard with an attentive eye every monument that remains of the characteriftics of their nature. Nor fhould the de- fire to retrieve, fo far as may be, every detail of the men and manners of that period, be dealt with as an idle inquifitivenefs, or ranked with that fpirit which, as Sir Thomas Browne relates, would feek to know what fong the Syrens fang, or by what name Achilles was known among the women.

If

If then we cannot prefent the lays of minftrels, who

> In fage and folemn tunes have fung
> Of turneys and of trophies hung ;
> Of forefts, and enchantments drear,
> Where more is meant than meets the ear ;

we can at leaft effay towards recovering the party lyrics with which the contending ranks of our great civil war folaced their friends or provoked their foes : and if there be any truth in the propofition of Fletcher of Saltoun, that the fongs of a people control its action not lefs than its laws, the production would be juftified of every ftrain that can be fhown to have been born out of the popular troubles of that day. There is a clafs of ftudents who would gladly hear all that can be told of every thing which went to form the character and the habits of the actors in the memorable fcene : to whom no fact, however fmall, that relates to the grand event of the Revolution, is deftitute of intereft : and to whofe eyes the words of the *Old Turcum* fong, that cheered the American camp-fires in the fwamps of Carolina fourfcore years bygone, would be not lefs precious today than the prefence of the finger himfelf would have been to Tarleton while the Britifh ftandard yet waved in Charlefton ; and thefe readers, at leaft, will not regard as altogether idle fuch collections as that here prefented.

In

In gathering up the poetry of the Revolution, a peculiar interest naturally attaches itself to the productions of the vanquished party. Of the sayings and doings of our own side, we may be presumed to possess at least a certain degree of information: but of the Tory or Loyal party, the general reader can hardly say more than that it was numerous, brave, and intelligent; and that when it was swept away from the face of the land, its members seem to have vanished from the public observation in the same moment with the cause which they had sustained. Like Cardinal Beaufort in the play, it died, and made no sign. The reader may, as he chooses, continue with Warwick, that so bad a death argued a monstrous life, or with the gentle king, lean to a milder judgment of the men who supported the cause of the crown. The question is of no moment here; and it is of as little importance to determine whether their literary effusions were possessed of any extraordinary merit. Their connection with the history of the times gives them value. The Englishman's boast, that he had sung the last Stuart out of three kingdoms loses none of its point because the verses themselves have but little, and every modern reader would resent the withdrawal from its appropriate place of the scurvy doggrel of *Lillibullero* as warmly as could have been done by My Uncle Toby himself, whose favorite resource in time of trouble, was, it will be recollected,

recollected, the whiftling of that Williamite air. It is their political rather than their lyrical merit that has caufed this collection of revolutionary verfes: and although, in the Editor's opinion, they are wanting in neither the one qualification nor the other, yet it may be as well on the latter fcore to premife that the reader muft not look to dealing with them fimply according to their poetical defert. "Ufe every man " after his defert," fays Hamlet, " and who fhould " 'fcape whipping ? Ufe them after your own honour " and dignity : the lefs they deferve, the more merit " is in your bounty. Take them in."

But notwithftanding all that has been advanced, it may ftill be doubted whether it was worth while to difturb the repofe of the pieces here printed. The Editor's intereft in a favorite line of refearch perhaps difqualified him for an unbiaffed decifion : and an appeal to the judgments of friends was about as profitable as that of John Bunyan in a like ftrait ;

> Some faid, John, print it : others faid, not fo.
> Some faid it may be good. Others faid No.

Accordingly, as is not unufual in fuch contingencies, he has followed the counfel that agreed beft with his own inclinations: fatiffied that the limited impreffion of this book will at leaft prevent any very widefpread diffatiffaction refulting from his proceedings.

In

In its preparation for the prefs, the Editor has been governed by the fame rules that controlled the appearance of *The Loyalift Poetry of the Revolution.* The Notes are made purely with an intent to explain the author's meaning. To maintain or to impugn the fentiments expreffed has been far from his plan. What incompletenefs appears in the Notes is as much to be regretted by himfelf as by any other; their hafty preparation under circumftances that left him accefs to no other authorities than what his own fhelves provided, may be fuggefted rather by way of explanation, than to juftify any deficiency. In the feleftion of the matter for the text of this work, however, it has been thought well to join together the names and the remaining compofitions of Doftor Odell and Mr. Stanfbury, who were undoubtedly the two moft important loyal verfifiers of the time. A concurrence of fortunate circumftances gave the Editor accefs to what may be reafonably believed a complete collection of all that remains of their writings. Many of thefe were unpublifhed; many in the original manufcript; and narrowed as their lift had already become under the hand of Time, there was every reafon to fuppofe they would continue to fuffer a yearly diminution. What eftimate may have been placed on them by the oppofing parties of the period in which they had birth, has not weighed at all to admit or exclude them from this collettion; nor have

have the opinions their language conveys been regarded. When party heats run high, party judgments are of little worth. "Wit and fool," fays Dryden, are confequents of Whig and Tory; and every man is a knave or an afs to the contrary fide. This arrangement indeed falls more feverely on the authors themfelves than upon any others: for it cannot be denied that their productions, as here given, are of very unequal merit and comprife much that, in all probability, they themfelves would on occafion have excluded. But the fault refts here with that Chance which, being no refpecter of merit, has preferved indifferently a meagre affortment, in point of quantity, of the numerous writings of our poets, and in fo doing has condemned their beft and their worft efforts to a fort of Mezentian union: *Mortua jungebat corpora vivis.* All that remains for the Editor under thefe circumftances is to fet in meet order and array the materials that he finds before him. Like Rob Roy, if they be 'ower bad for blefling, they are ower gude for banning:' and the moft careleffly arranged line may perhaps be found to illuftrate fome neglected point of hiftory.

Efpecial acknowledgments are due to Mrs. Charles Lee, of Frederickton, N. B., and to Mr. J. Francis Fifher and Mr. Charles M. Morris of Philadelphia, for their contributions to the text of this volume. The Editor would alfo remark here that from it he has

omitted

omitted two poems by Doctor Odell: *The American Times*, and *The Word of Congress*—which are already edited in *The Loyalist Poetry.* To the critical reader, who may object to the occafional omiffion of a phrafe allowable enough in the laft century, but too coarfe for the more delicate palate of this, he would urge that in every fuch cafe a dafh has been fubftituted for the difcarded word; fo, in the language of Peter Pindar,

—Let *thy* impudence fupply the rhyme !

W. S.

Glofter Place, Miffiffippi,
   January 10th, 1860.

C

CONTENTS.

Table of Contents. xxi

THE

LOYAL VERSES

OF

STANSBURY AND ODELL.

THE

LOYAL VERSES

OF

STANSBURY AND ODELL.

A SONG,

SUNG AT THE SECOND ANNIVERSARY MEETING OF THE
SONS OF ST. GEORGE IN NEW YORK, APRIL 23, 1771.

TUNE: *Black Sloven.*

[From Joſeph Stanſbury's Original MSS.[1]]

YE Sons of St. George, here aſſembled today,
So honeſt and hearty, ſo Chearful and Gay,
Come join in the Chorus, and loyally ſing
In praiſe of your Patron, Your Country and King.

Tho'plac'd at a diſtance from Britain's bold Shore,
From thence either We or our Fathers came o'er:
And in Will, Word and Deed, We are Engliſhmen all;
Still true to her Cauſe and awake to her Call.

Let

Let Creffy, Poictiers, and let Agincourt show
How our Anceftors acted fome Ages ago:
While Minden's red Field and Quebec shall proclaim
That their Sons are unchanged or in Nature or Name.

Should the proud Spanifh Dons but appear on the Main,
The Ifland they pilfer'd, by Force to maintain,
The brave Sons of Thunder our Wrongs will redrefs,
And teach them again what they learn'd of Queen Befs.

Tho' the proud Roman Eagle to Britain was borne,
Both Talons and Feathers got plaguily torn;
And Cæfar himfelf, both with Foot and with Horfe,
Was glad to fneak off with—"It's well 'twas no worfe."

Tho' party Contentions awhile may run high,
When Danger advances they'll vanifh and die;
While all with one Heart, Hand and Spirit unite,
Like Englifhmen think and like Englifhmen fight.

Then here's to our King, and Oh, Long may He reign—
The Lord of thofe Men who are Lords of the Main!
While all the Contention among us fhall be
To make Him as happy as We are made free.

And here's to the Daughters of Britain's Fair Ifle—
May Freedom and They ever crown with a Smile
The Sons of St. George, our good Knight fo profound—
The Sons of St. George, even all the World round!

ON

ON THE PRESENT TROUBLES.

[Theſe Lines from the Stanſbury Manuſcripts, have an intereſt as ſhowing how ſome even among thoſe who, when War actually broke out, were unflinching in their Loyalty to the Crown,
were at an earlier date diſguſted with the miniſterial plans for
America. The author's confidence in the overwhelming Power
of England is curiouſly enough contraſted with his aſſertion of
Colonial Innocence.[2]]

O N cryſtal throne, uplifted high,
  Imperial Britain ſate ;
Her lofty forehead reach'd the ſky ;
  Her awful nod was fate :
Terrific Mars, with War's alarms
  Augments the pageant ſhew ;
And ſea-green Neptune's circling arms
  Forbid th' invading foe.

Bright Science made her Name ador'd.
  Her robes the Arts empearl'd.
Wide in her Lap fair Commerce pour'd
  The Riches of the World.
Her Cheeks the Roſe in haſte forſook,
  By jealous Fears purſued :
Her Voice the Earth's firm Baſement ſhook,
  And turn'd the Air to Blood.

Her Vengeance o'er the liquid Wave
  Explores theſe weſtern Climes :
Juſt Heav'n ! a People deign to ſave
  Whoſe wrongs are all their Crimes !
   Cetera deſunt.

WHEN

WHEN GOOD QUEEN ELIZABETH GOVERNED THE REALM.

𝔄 𝔖𝔬𝔫𝔤.

TUNE: *Hearts of Oak.*

[From the Stanſbury Manuſcripts; and probably compoſed for a meeting of the Sons of St. George in 1774 or 1775.]

WHEN good Queen Elizabeth govern'd the
    Realm,
And Burleigh's ſage Counſels directed the Helm,
In vain Spain and France our Conqueſts oppoſ'd;
For Valour conducted what Wiſdom propoſ'd.
        Beef and Beer was their Food;
        Love and Truth arm'd their Band;
        Their Courage was ready—
        Steady, Boys, Steady—
To fight and to conquer by Sea and by Land.

But ſince Tea and Coffee, ſo much to our Grief,
Have taken the place of Strong Beer and Roaſt Beef,
Our Laurels have wither'd, our Trophies been torn;
And the Lions of England French triumphs adorn.
        Tea and ſlops are their food;
        They unnerve every Hand—
        Their Courage unſteady
        And not always ready—
They often are conquer'd by Sea and by Land.

St. George views with Tranſport our generous flame:
" My Sons, riſe to Glory, and rival my fame.
" Ancient Manners again in my Sons I behold

                    And

"And this Age muft eclipfe all the Ages of Gold."[3]
        Beef and Beer are our food;
        Love and Truth Arm our Band;
        Our Courage is fteady
        And always is ready
To fight and to conquer by Sea and by Land.

While thus we regale as our Fathers of old,
Our Manners as Simple, our Courage as bold,
May Vigour and Prudence our Freedom fecure
Long as Rivers, or Ocean, or Stars fhall endure.
        Beef and Beer are our food;
        Love and Truth arm our Band;
        Our Courage is fteady,
        And always is ready
To fight and to conquer by Sea and by Land.

———

INSCRIPTION

FOR A CURIOUS CHAMBER-STOVE, IN THE FORM OF AN
URN, SO CONTRIVED AS TO MAKE THE FLAME DESCEND,
INSTEAD OF RISE, FROM THE FIRE: INVENTED BY
DOCTOR FRANKLIN.

[By Dr. JONATHAN ODELL.[4] 1776.]

LIKE a Newton fublimely he foar'd
    To a Summit before unattained;
New regions of Science explor'd,
    And the Palm of Philofophy gain'd.

With a Spark, that he caught from the Skies,
    He difplay'd an unparallel'd wonder:
And we faw, with delight and furprife,
    That his Rod could protect us from thunder.

                                   O

O had he been wife to purfue
The track for his talents defign'd,
What a tribute of praife had been due
To the teacher and friend of Mankind!

But to covet *political* fame
Was, in him, a degrading ambition;
A Spark, that from *Lucifer* came,
And kindled the blaze of *Sedition*.

Let Candor, then, write on his Urn—
Here lies the renowned Inventor,
Whofe flame to the Skies ought to burn,
But, inverted, defcends to the Center!

EPIGRAM

ON A SERMON PREACHED BY THE REV. MR. PIERCY, CHAPLAIN TO THE THIRD BATTALION OF PHILADELPHIA MILITIA.

[By JOSEPH STANSBURY. The late Rev. Dr. James Abercrombie, Rector of the united Parifhes of Chrift-church and St. Peter's, in Philadelphia (for notices of whom fee *Croker's Bofwell's Johnfon*, vol. III, p. 242, p. 285), who communicated this piece, could not fix its date, but believed it to have been written in June or July, 1776. "The weather being very warm," faid Dr. Abercrombie, "the fervant of General Roberdeau (who commanded the battalion), a very black and remarkably ugly Negro, ftood behind Mr. Percy, in the pulpit, fanning him with a degree of vehemence proportioned to his inflammatory addrefs."[5]]

TO preach up, friend Percy, at this critical feafon,
Refiftance to Britain, is not very civil.
Yet what can we look for but Faction and Treafon
From a flaming Enthufiaft, fann'd by the Devil?

BIRTHDAY

BIRTHDAY ODE.

[Written by Dr. ODELL, on occaſion of the King's Birthday, June 4th, 1776; and ſung by a number of Britiſh officers (captured at St. John's and Chambly by General Montgomery) who were priſoners at that time at Burlington, New Jerſey; and who, to avoid offence, had an entertainment in honor of the day prepared on an iſland in the river Delaware, where they dined under a tree.[6] Printed from the author's copy, collated with a contemporaneous Manuſcript.]

O'ER Britannia's happy Land,
Rul'd by George's mild command,
On this bright, auſpicious day
Loyal hearts their tribute pay.
Ever ſacred be to mirth
The day that gave our Monarch birth!

There, the thundering Cannon's roar
Echoes round from ſhore to ſhore;
Royal Banners wave on high;
Drums and trumpets rend the ſky.

There our Comrades clad in Arms,
Long enured to War's alarms,
Marſhall'd all in bright array
Welcome this returning day.

There, the temples chime their bells;
And the pealing anthem ſwells;
And the gay, the grateful throng
Join the loud triumphant ſong!

Nor

The Loyal Verses

Nor to Britain's Isle confin'd—
Many a distant Region join'd
Under George's happy sway
Joys to hail this welcome day.

O'er this Land among the rest,
Till of late supremely blest,
George, to sons of Britain dear,
Swell'd the song from year to year.

Here, we now lament to find
Sons of Britain, fierce and blind,
Drawn from loyal love astray,
Hail no more this welcome day.

When by foreign Foes dismay'd,
Thankless Sons, ye call'd for aid:
Then, *we* gladly fought and bled,
And your Foes in triumph led.

Now, by Fortune's blind command,
Captives in your hostile Land;
To this lonely spot we stray
Here unseen to hail this day!

Though by Fortune thus betray'd,
For a while we seek the shade,
Still our loyal hearts are free—
Still devoted, George, to thee!

Britain, Empress of the Main,
Fortune envies thee in vain:
Safe, while Ocean round thee flows,
Though the *world* were *all* thy Foes.

                                    Long

Long as Sun and Moon endure
Britain's Throne fhall ftand fecure,
And great George's royal line
There in fplendid honor fhine.
  Ever facred be to Mirth
  The day that gave our Monarch birth!

————

SONG

FOR A FISHING PARTY NEAR BURLINGTON, ON THE
DELAWARE, IN 1776.

[Compofed by Dr. ODELL, under circumftances fimilar to
thofe which occafioned the preceding piece. To the third verfe
he has appended this Note : " *Proteftant* was a term adopted by
a circle of Loyalifts."]

HOW fweet is the feafon, the fky how ferene;
 On Delaware's banks how delightful the fcene;
The Prince of the Rivers, his waves all afleep,
In filence majeftic glides on to the Deep.

Away from the noife of the Fife and the Drum,
And all the rude din of Bellona we come;
And a plentiful ftore of good humor we bring
To feafon our feaft in the fhade of Cold Spring.

A truce then to all whig and tory debate;
True lovers of Freedom, contention we hate :
For the Demon of difcord in vain tries his art
To poffefs or inflame a true *Proteftant* heart.

True

True Proteſtant friends to fair Liberty's cauſe,
To decorum, good order, religion and laws,
From avarice, jealouſy, perfidy, free;
We wiſh all the world were as happy as we.

We have wants, we confeſs, but are free from the care
Of thoſe that abound, yet have nothing to ſpare:
Serene as the ſky, as the river ſerene,
We are happy to want envy, malice and ſpleen.

While thouſands around us, miſled by a few,
The Phantoms of pride and ambition purſue,
With pity their fatal deluſion we ſee;
And wiſh all the world were as happy as we!

A WELCOME TO HOWE.

[Written by JOSEPH STANSBURY, on occaſion of the arrival of
Sir William Howe on the coaſt of New York, in June, 1776.]

HE comes, he comes, the Hero comes:
Sound, ſound your Trumpets, beat your Drums:
From port to port let Cannon roar
Howe's welcome to this weſtern Shore!

Britannia's dauntleſs Sons appear;
For Ages paſt renown'd in War.
The Sword they draw, the Lance they wield,
Now Glory calls them to the Field.

With laurels crown'd triumphant ſee
Britannia's Genius, Victory:
With her, fair Freedom ſits in State,
And Mercy ſmiles, ſerenely great.

My

My Sons, Britannia cries—forbear:
Deluded Sons, nor urge the War.
What Juſtice aſks, is all your own;
For Juſtice yet ſupports my Throne.

Would you be free?—be Freedom thine:
Britannia bends at Freedom's ſhrine.
Is Wealth your Wiſh?—that Wealth poſſeſs,
For Britain's King delights to bleſs.

Be happy ſtill, nor dare explore
With moon-ſtruck Guides the heights of Pow'r:
For Pow'r is mine, and flows from me
In temper'd Streams of Liberty.

With me connected, ſtand ſecure
While Sun or Moon or Stars endure:
And when the World is wrapt in Fire,
This mighty Empire laſt expire.

A BIRTHDAY SONG.

[By Dr. ODELL: compoſed at New York, in honour of the anniverſary of the King's birthday, June 4th, 1777; and printed in the Gentleman's Magazine for that year.]

TIME was when America hallow'd the morn
   On which the lov'd monarch of Britain was born,
Hallow'd the day, and joyfully chanted
      God ſave the King!
Then flouriſh'd the bleſſings of freedom and peace,
And plenty flow'd in with a yearly increaſe.
Proud of our lot we chanted merrily
      Glory and joy crown the King!

With

With envy beheld by the nations around,
We rapidly grew, nor was anything found
Able to check our growth while we chanted
      God ſave the King!
O bleſt beyond meaſure, had honour and truth
Still nurſ'd in our hearts what they planted in youth!
Loyalty ſtill had chanted merrily
      Glory and joy crown the King!

But ſee! how rebellion has lifted her head!
How honour and truth are with loyalty fled!
Few are there now who join us in chanting
      God ſave the King!
And ſee! how deluded the multitude fly
To arm in a cauſe that is built on a lye!
Yet are we proud to chant thus merrily
      Glory and joy crown the King!

Though faction by falſehood awhile may prevail,
And loyalty ſuffers a captive in jail,
Britain is rouz'd, rebellion is falling:
      God ſave the King!
The captive ſhall ſoon be releaſ'd from his chain;
And conqueſt reſtore us to Britain again,
Ever to join in chanting merrily
      Glory and joy crown the King!

                    TRADESMEN'S

TRADESMEN'S SONG

FOR HIS MAJESTY'S BIRTH DAY, JUNE 4TH, 1777.

TUNE: *When Britain firſt at Heaven's command.*

[By JOSEPH STANSBURY, and firſt printed in the Pennſylvania Ledger, October 22d, 1777. The Ledger was a tory paper, iſſued weekly by James Humphreys, at Philadelphia, during Sir William Howe's occupation of that city. On the 4th of June the city was ſtill occupied by the Whigs, and this ſong could not have obtained publicity before Howe's arrival without bringing trouble on its author's head.

AGAIN, my ſocial Friends, we meet
    To celebrate our annual Treat,
And with our loyal hearts diſplay
This great, this glorious Natal Day :
    'Tis George's Natal Day we ſing ;
    Our firm, our ſteady Friend and King.

For Britain's Parliament and Laws
He waves his own Imperial Power ;
For this (Old England's glorious Cauſe)
May Heaven on him its bleſſings ſhower ;
    And Colonies, made happy, ſing
    Great George, their real Friend and King.

Since Britain firſt at Heaven's command
Aroſe from out the Azure Main,
Did ever o'er this jarring Land
A Monarch with more firmneſs reign ?
    Then to the Natal Day we'll ſing
    Of George, our ſacred Friend and King.

To

To Charlotte fair, our matchlefs Queen,
To all his blooming, heavenly line,
To all their Family and Friends
Let us in hearty chorus join:
    And George's Natal Day let's fing,
    Our gracious Father, Friend and King.[7]

And may the heavenly Powers combine,
While we with loyal hearts implore
That one of his moft facred Line
May rule thefe Realms till Time's no more:
    And we with chearful voices fing
    Great George our fteady, natal King.

———

THE FOURTH OF JULY.

1777.

[R. CHUBB is the reputed author of thefe lines: but as they have alfo been attributed to STANSBURY, the editor with fome hefitation gives them a place here. They are printed from the Pennfylvania Ledger of December 10th, 1777; collated with a manufcript copy. The text in the Ledger is prefaced by this Note: "The following was written in commemoration of the *glorious action* on the evening of the 4th of July laft, when a party of *courageous Independents*, headed by fome of their Rebel Chiefs, waged a moft daring war againft the unenlightened windows of the Quakers and other enemies to their ridiculous independent fcheme in this city."[8]]

WHAT times are thefe?—a perfect riddle!
    Whence fled the fcenes of former quiet?
Blefs us—when Patriots ftrum the fiddle,
    And Generals form and head the riot!

The

The unarm'd Quakers and the Tories
 Suftained the honours of the night,
And ftill their poor, unfhutter'd ftories
 Hang zig-zag trophies of their might.

See General Gates and Dicky Peters,[9]
 With Jemmy Meafe of noted worth;[10]
Richard and Tom the prime of eaters,
 Like ancient heroes fally forth.[11]

Our true Don Quixotes, by falfe gueffings
 Direct their calls and lead the van:
Miftake the Tories for the Heffians,
 And Quaker for poor Englifhman!

Illuftrious Chieftains! future ages
 Shall mark your triumphs of the day.
While wide the patriotic Sages
 Shall round the world your fame convey.

Still as a foil, ye new Law-makers,
 To former happinefs remain.
Blunderers, go on: defpife the Quakers—
 You never fhall their heighth attain.[12]

The wifdom of their gentle ruling
 Can bear the retrofpective view;
And this, with all your boafted fchooling,
 Is more than will be faid of you.

         A

A NEW SONG.

TUNE: *Cæsar and Pompey were both of them*, &c.

[By Mr. STANSBURY: printed from the original Manuscript.[13]]

WHEN Britain determined to tax us at pleasure,
We rose as one Man, and opposed the measure;
Not liking the Pilgrimage, I can assure ye,
Of going to England for Trial by Jury.[14]
     Therefore for Freedom alone we are fighting;
     For that sort of Freedom was not so inviting.

To Edicts of Britain subjection refusing,
We set up a Government of our own chusing.
The Guardians of Freedom resolv'd to maintain it,
And publish'd a long Bill of Rights to explain it.
    For its for Freedom alone we are fighting:
    The name of all names which true Freemen delight in.

We fondly imagin'd that all future Story
Should tell of our Justice, our Freedom and Glory:
We laugh'd at Oppression, not dreaming or fearing
That Men would be banish'd without charge or hearing:
    For Freedom indeed we suppofed we were fighting;
    But this fort of Freedom's not very inviting.

If they with our Enemies have been partakers,
Then prove it in God's name, and punish the Quakers:
But if there is nothing alleged but Suspicion,
What honest Man's safe from this State-Inquisition?
    If such be the Freedom for which we are fighting,
    This sample, good Folks, is not very inviting.
                      When

When good Men are feiz'd on, who boldly defie all
The malice of Hell, and demand a fair Trial —
The caufe of refufal you vainly diffemble:
" The Churchmen muft bend, and the Quakers fhall
    tremble."
  Since this is the Freedom for which we are fighting,
  The old-fafhioned Freedom was much more inviting.

When Quakers and Churchmen have fuffer'd your
    pleafure—
Their Worfhip and Confciences fhap'd to your mea-
    fure—
The Catholics then may expect Penal Laws,
Whereby we fhall have one Religion and Caufe.[15]
  This, this is the Freedom for which you are fighting:
  And let all who think it so, call it inviting.

———

THE PETITION OF PHILADELPHIA TO SIR WILLIAM HOWE.

[Written by Mr. STANSBURY, about October, 1777, and now
printed from his revifed manufcript copy, collated with the rough
draft. The latter, by the way, fupplies the names of *Price* and
Coffin in the thirtieth line.[16]]

TO General Howe, Commiffioner in chief
    To grant all injured Subjects *fure Relief*,
We, the Subfcribers, beg leave to prefent
This State of Facts, by way of — *Compliment*:

That long before the date of Whig and Tory
The *Paper-Money* was this Country's Glory;
In all our Dealings did its Value hold
In fix'd *Proportion* to the Coins of Gold:—

  3   That

That when the Britifh Troops firft took Poffeffion
It paff'd as formerly by your Conceffion :—
That with the Fleet came up the *Merchant-Stranger*,
Who, by refufing, brought *it* into danger: ·
(Inform'd perhaps that ftill in Rebel's hands
Lay all the mortgage-Deeds and mortgag'd Lands,
And reaf'ning thence have fo miftook the Cafe
They hold the Money's tottering as *its bafe*)   .
And certain *Citizens*, we muft confefs it t'ye,
Have brought their Brethren into fad neceffity.

That if fuppreft, it may be mildly faid
We have no *Medium* adequate to Trade ;
And if the Army fell their Bills at all
Th' Exchange they fell at muft be very fmall.

That *it* received the *Sanction of the Crown :*
And many *Friends of Government* in Town,
Sold each *Half-Joe* for *Twelve Pounds*, Congrefs Trafh,
Which purchaf'd *Six Pounds* of this Legal Cafh ;
Whereby they have, if you will bar the bubble,
Inftead of lofing, *made their Money double :*
Then pity them, the widow and the orphan—
Nor heed the partial Tale from Price or Coffin.

That in the Year (the famous) Fifty-Nine—
A Year which muft in Britain's Annals fhine—[17]
The Army *wanting Cafh* obtain'd the Loan
Of Paper Money, Fifty Thoufand Pounds :
By which their Bills, that fcarce a Man would buy,
Advanc'd *Fourteen per Cent* immediately.
Its true the Army now has Cafh enough ;
And *therefore* fhould fupport our Paper Stuff.

That a *large Sum*, collected with difpatch,
Lays in the Treaf'rers hands to pay the *Watch*,
Who will *not take it*, unlefs in the Shops
And Market it will buy them Food and Slops.

Our

Our Patrole *therefore* will have *Guns and Swords*,
Inſtead of Lanthorns, Staves, and empty Words.[18]
   That if you will aſſume our Load of *Ills*,
Our Paper's *ready* to exchange for *Bills*,
To pay our Friends in England with your *Gold*,
And leave your Officers our *Rags* to hold.
   Theſe and *more cogent* Reaſons might be told
Why Paper Money ſhould be par with Gold.

   We pray the General in a general Way
Would grant Redreſs, and that without Delay,
And *Value* give the *Paper* we poſſeſs : —
And then—*We'll ſign the long-ſince penn'd Addreſs.*[19]

EPIGRAM.

["Wrote extempore by JOSEPH STANSBURY on ſeeing a thin,
Sieve-like Blanket returned by General Howe, in lieu of a good
Roſe Swanſkin, taken from a Quaker."[20]]

WHEN Congreſs had fled in a Fright from their
         Foes,
The Quakers they thought to ſnug under the *Roſe*.
But *Billy*, who ſees with the Glance of an Eye,
Soon found though the Quakers were grave, they were
         ſly :
Reſolv'd to diſtinguiſh the *good* from the *bad*,
I'll ſift 'em, he cries, if there's ſieves to be had !

                                    THE

THE KITTEN SONG.

TUNE: *Come my kitten, my kitten,* &c.

[Probably by Mr. STANSBURY: publiſhed in Towne's Pennſylvania Evening Poſt, December 2d, 1777, with this prefatory Note:
"*Good Mr. Towne*—You muſt have heard of the aſſociation or
agreement that the ladies of this city (Philadelphia) have entered
into, in order to ſupport the old paper currency which has received
the ſanction of our gracious ſovereign; and of their determination
to exert themſelves, as far as ladies can, to reſtore it to its former
value. Now you muſt know, Sir, I am a ſubſcriber to that
agreement, and being myſelf vaſtly fond of a little fun and harmleſs humour, have concluded, from your phyſiognomy, that you
have no objection to either, I have therefore ſent you a new
ſong to an old tune. By inſerting it in your next paper, you will
oblige a number of ladies, and among the reſt your conſtant reader,
Flirtilla. Philad. Dec. 1, 1777." In many reſpects theſe lines
will remind the reader of the childiſh nurſery doggerel that ſupplies the air: but the circumſtances under which they were compoſed conſtitute an intereſting feature in the local hiſtory of the
day.21]

COME all ye good people attend
  Pray hear what a new comer offers;
I've all ſorts of good things to vend,
  If you will but open your coffers.
    Here we go up, up, up,
      And here we go down, down-e;
    Here we go backwards and forwards
      And here we go round, round, round-e!

Here

Here is a fleet from New York,
    And here the dry goods ſhall abound-e;
Here is both butter and pork,
    And all juſt now come round-e.

Here you have ſalt for your broth,
    And here you have ſugar and cheeſe-e;
Tea without taxes or oath,
    But down with your *gold*, if you pleaſe-e.

Here is an end to your rags,
    Your backs ſhall no more go bare-e:
Farewell to the ſneers of the wags,
    But your *gold*, Sir, muſt firſt take air-e.

Here you have good Iriſh beef,
    And here you have ſugar and ſpice-e;
Here you may part with your grief,
    For *gold* we have plumbs for mince pies-e.

Here you have topknot and *tête*
    Too big for a buſhel to hold-e;
Here you may dreſs like the great:
    And all for a trifle of gold-e.

Here you have catgut and gauze,
    And cambrick and lawn very fine-e;
Mits, hoſe, and a thouſand kickſhaws,
    For which let your *silver* be mine-e.

Here you have trinkets so fine,
    And baubles to hang by your ſide-e;
Here you may glitter and ſhine;
    For *gold* you may look like a bride-e.

                                    Then

Then fpurn at the wife old dons,
    Who make for their *paper* a rout-e;
Here's goods for your *gold* at once;
    Come, out with your *gold*, come out-e.

You'll ruin the land, we know,
    By joining with what we've told-e:
But fince all your wealth muft go,
    We'll ftrive to encircle your gold-e.

Come, furely I've told you enough!
    We have all that you want and wifh-e;
But pray give us no paper ftuff:
    We come for the loaf and the fifh-e.
        Here we go up, up, up,
            And here we go down, down-e;
        Here we go backwards and forwards
            And here we go round, round, round-e!

————

VERSES TO THE TORIES.

[By Mr. STANSBURY. Thefe lines appear to have been
written in confideration of the hardfhips endured by perfons who
on the charge of being inimically difpofed towards the interefts of
America, had been taken into cuftody by the Whigs, and confined in fome interior and remote town.22]

COME, ye brave, by Fortune wounded
    More than by the vaunting Foe,
Chear your hearts, ne'er be confounded;
Trials all muft undergo.
Tho' without or Rhyme or Reafon
Hurried back thro' Wilds unknown,

                                    Virtue's

Virtue's ſmiles can make a Priſon
Far more charming than a Throne.
Think not, tho' wretched, poor, or naked,
Your breaſt alone the Load ſuſtains:
Sympathizing Hearts partake it—
Britain's Monarch ſhares your Pains.
This Night of Pride and Folly over,
A dawn of Hope will ſoon appear.
In its light you ſhall diſcover
Your triumphant day is near.

THE CARPET KNIGHT.

[This piece, collated from two of Mr. Stanſbury's Manuſcripts, offers a renewed evidence of the diſeſteem into which Sir
William Howe fell during his occupation of Philadelphia. The
Tories were ſurprized and diſguſted at ſeeing his fine army unem-
ployed in any ſerious enterpriſe, and his ſplendid military capaci-
ties yielding to ſlothfulneſs, diſſipation and extravagance; and,
as many thought, even to avarice. The mortal whoſe charms
were preferred, according to the ſong, to thoſe of Venus herſelf,
was probably a married lady from Jamaica Plains, near Boſton,
who is named in this ſame connection, but in rather broader phraſe,
by Francis Hopkinſon, in his *Battle of the Kegs.* The date of
this ſong ſeems to be December 24th, 1777; ſhortly after Howe's
return to the city from his idle attempt to ſurpriſe Waſhington's
Army at Whitemarſh.23]

LATE a Council of Gods from their heavenly abodes
  Were call'd on Olympus to meet;
Jove gave his commands from his throne in the clouds:
  Attend, and his words I'll repeat.

Ye

Ye know, all ye Pow'rs that attend my high Throne,
    Your Will to my Pleafure muft bow:
I will, that thofe Gifts which you prize as your own,
    Shall now be beftow'd on my *Howe.*

Aftræa, who long fince had quitted the Earth,
    Prefented her Balance and Sword ;
The Honors derived from Titles and Birth
    By *Juno* were inftant conferred ;
Fierce *Mars* gave his Chariot ; gay *Hermes* his Wand;
    Alcides, his Club and his Bow ;
Sweet *Peace* with her Olive-branch graced his hand ;
    And *Venus,* herfelf did beftow.

Thus, enrich'd with fuch Gifts as the Gods can impart,
    The Hero by *Jove* was addreff'd :
As you wifh to reclaim each American heart,
    Let Juftice prefide in your breaft ;
Exhibit the bleffings of Order and Peace
    As wide as your Conquefts fhall fpread ;
Let your Promife be facred — Rebellion fhall ceafe,
    And the Laurel fhall bloom round your head. ·

I know that fell *Difcord,* your zeal to oppofe,
    Will nourifh Sedition and Hate :
Miftakes may occur, and Friends fuffer with Foes :
    Yet your Wifh is confirmed by Fate.[24] ·
Sweet Peace fhall revive from the horrors of War ;
    Her Empire again be reftor'd ;
Affection and Duty fhall cover each Scar,
    And *Howe* by the World be ador'd !

Now with fhame muft the Mufe the fad fequel difplay;
    With Sorrow, and Shame, and Surprife :
The Gifts of *Aftræa* he loft by the way,
    And her fillet he plac'd o'er his Eyes.

                              The

The Arms of *Alcides* he ſent to Burgoyne,
 And with them the Chariot of *Mars:*
For what but Aſſiſtance and Weapons divine
 Could finiſh ſuch Quixotic Wars?

Hermes' Wand was now uſeleſs; no Snakes would unite:
 The Olive in vain was diſplay'd;
For bleſſings no longer attended the fight,
 And Loyalty fled from its ſhade.[25]
The Gifts ſent to Burgoyne return'd to the ſkies—
 Deſpairing he yielded his Arms:
And fair *Venus*, diſguſted, beheld with Surprize
 A Mortal preferr'd to her Charms.

A FABLE.

[Printed from Mr. Stanſbury's Manuſcript, and bearing date
January 24th, 1778.]

IN antient Times, the Poets ſing,
 The Lion was elected King;
And all the Beaſts, with homage due,
Proffer'd and ſwore allegiance true
To him and to his heirs forever;
And ſo far all went ſmooth and clever.

But his dominions were ſo large,
He could not execute his charge
And give his ſubjects that protection
He promiſ'd them on his election,
Unleſs he call'd in ſome aſſiſtance:
For Brutes, as Men, will make reſiſtance }
To lawful Kings, when at a diſtance.

4

And

And, as he rul'd with feebleſt ſway
Where Pennyfeather's Foreſts lay,
He named the Leopard, Greyhound, Fox,
To hold them as with Bolts and Locks ;
Three truſty Brutes to act together
As joint Viceroys o'er Pennyfeather.

Some time the project ſeemed to anſwer.
All day the happy Beaſts could dance, or
Sing and play a thouſand tricks ;
Make bows or cringes ; jump o'er ſticks ;
And do what in their power lay
To pleaſe the Brutes who bore the Sway.
The Viceroys made ſuch large Profeſſions
Of guarding every Brute's poſſeſſions,
As private Virtue, public Zeal,
The good of all the Common Weal,
Alone inſpir'd their patriot Wiſh :—
No diſtant view of Loaf or Fiſh.
All ſelf and ſelfiſh aims ſubdued,
They lived but for the common good.

True Patriots are indeed a rarity ;
And yet I may in truth declare it t'ye,
They dealt their Cards ſo well about
That no one entertain'd a doubt
But *Juſtice* had reſign'd her throne,
And left her Scales with them alone.

The tale proceeds : Upon the ground
An Oſtritch Egg one day was found,
By ſhipwreck caſt upon the ſhore.
The Beaſts the prize in triumph bore,
And laid it at their ruler's feet
With honour and obedience meet.

I

———— I muſt not dwell
Too long upon this precious ſhell.
What—but an Egg to be divided!
How can this buſineſs be decided!

Why, cries the Fox, this lucky Stroke
May be improved—the Egg's unbroke—
Then inſtant place it on the Strand,
And careful cover it with Sand;
Expoſe it to the Sun's warm beam,
And ſoon the Egg with Life will teem;
Produce a Bird of monſtrous ſize
And weight and worth—a glorious Prize!
A Prize which we will ſhare together,
Nor throw away a ſingle Feather.

Sir Fox, cries Leopard, ſure you joke,
Nor think how 'twill the Beaſts provoke.
We rule with delegated Powers;
They think the Prize is theirs, not ours.
Oh, how our Cheeks will burn with Shame
When they traduce our public Fame,
And every Raſcal cries at pleaſure—" he
" Is one of thoſe that robb'd the Treaſury,
" And ſmuggled to himſelf the Gold
" For which the Egg ſhould have been ſold."
Let my advice this time prevail:
Expoſe the Egg to public Sale:
And whatſoe'er it ſhall produce,
Apply it to the public uſe.

The Greyhound pauſ'd—then thus began:
I much approve the Leopard's plan.
What he obſerves is very true;
The Rabble think the Egg their due,

And

And would with endleſs noiſe and clatter
Purſue us, if we ſmugg'd the matter.
What we *ſhould* do is mighty plain :
What we may do, I'll juſt explain.
We may amuſe the Beaſts who crave it,
And ſay — the higheſt bid ſhall have it.
But few of them have ſeen ſuch Fowl,
Or know an Oſtrich from an owl.
Afraid the Bird may ſhortly die,
They'll cautious be, nor bid too high :
And thoſe who know its worth and uſe,
Will ſwear they would prefer a Gooſe,
Or Hen that lays good ſtore of Eggs :
That bating Feathers, Neck and Legs,
It was no larger than a Widgeon,
Nor half ſo fat as good Squab Pidgeon.
Then make a Bid with careleſs Air —
Not half its Value, you may ſwear.
Hence we may take a fair Occaſion
And ſerve, each one, his own Relation,
In ſuch a way, the candid muſt
And will acknowledge, ſtrictly juſt.
Let's inſtant pay the higheſt price —
The Matter's ſettled in a trice —
And give our Friends the Egg to nurſe ;
The Public's ſerv'd — who fares the worſe ?
Pray, why may not our Puppies claim
Their honeſt ſhare of Wealth or Fame,
And fill in time the higher claſſes ?
And, cloathed with honor, be juſt Aſſes ?

The Speech produc'd a general Smile :
And 'twas agreed to ſhare the Spoil.

ON

ON THE DOWNFALL OF LEGAL PAPER MONEY.

[Written at Philadelphia in the winter of 1777-8, by Mr. STANSBURY, and printed from a collation of his reviſed manuſcript copy with the rough draft. From the alluſion in the ſixteenth line, the piece would ſeem to have been addreſſed to Rev. Dr. William Smith, whoſe oration on the death of General Montgomery (Feb. 19th, 1776) was long conſidered a model of patriotic eloquence. Literary taſtes and a common religion may have eſtabliſhed a congeniality between Dr. Smith and the author which political prejudices need not have deſtroyed.26]

WHEN Charles's Horſe, for want of Breath,
   Like others fell a prey to Death,
No courtier dar'd to raiſe his head,
And tell the News, "that he was dead."
At laſt they fix'd on Killigrew—
For what may not a Jeſter do?
A licenſ'd Wag, who, ſpite of Rule,
Will ſpeak bold Truths and play the Fool,
And tell a Monarch to his face
His Horſe is dead, if ſuch the caſe.

In pride of War, when Heroes fall,
Then—Eloquence ſhould grace the Pall;
In nervous Style their Worth proclaim;
And fix them on the rolls of Fame
In patriot ſtrains, devoid of flummery,
Like your Oration on Montgomery.27

No Hero's praiſes claim my Song;
No praiſe is due to acting wrong:

'To

To burning, ſtripping, cheating, plundering:
Delays, Miſtakes and endleſs blundering:
Nor Charles's German horſe that's dead:
But faith, it is the *Want of Bread*,
Which threatens hard, (look e'er ſo funny)
Since the deceaſe of Paper Money.[28]

Seiz'd by a Fit of Oppoſition
Which baffled ev'ry State Phyſician;
Each lenient Meaſure tried in vain
To bring her back to Health again;
Her nerves ſo firm and weak by ſpells;[29]
It poſed the Doctors Smith and Wells:
And when they order'd ſtronger Med'cines
She languiſh'd —puked—in fine, is dead ſince.

Ah! what avails her former Pride,
When buſy Commerce roll'd his tide
Obedient to her nod? Her ſmile
Richly repaid the Lab'rers toil.
The regal Crown, with Splendor bright,
From her has aſk'd, and borrow'd Light.
Ah! what avails the Peaſant's cry:
The tatter'd Veſt: the aſking Eye:
The famiſh'd Look! the aking Heart:
The Infant's ſcream: the Parent's ſmart:
The fainting Wife: the Friend expiring,
For want of Food and Cloaths and Firing!

In this ſad Caſe, *Humanity* muſt fail,
Nor *Charity* can ſave the Wretch from Jail!
Both want the means to eaſe the victim's Woe,
Since *Gold* is Wealth, and *Paper* only Shew.
With heartfelt Sorrow then inſcribe her Urn,
And bid Poſterity the Story mourn.

INSCRIPTION.

INSCRIPTION.

Here reſts, in hope ſome future Day to riſe
With former Luſtre in theſe weſtern Skies,
A Heap of Paper, once by Britain made
The Life of Commerce, Agriculture, Trade ;
The Sign of Wealth, and all that Wealth could grant ;
The Friend of Man, the Antidote of Want !

Tho' by Rebellion now entomb'd awhile,
This ſeeming lifeleſs Heap again ſhall ſmile ;
Again revive—exert her native Fire—
And ſhall with Britain flouriſh or expire !

ODE

FOR THE YEAR 1778.

[Printed from a contemporaneous Manuſcript, and believed to
have been written by Mr. STANSBÚRY.]

WHEN rival nations, great in arms,
　　Great in power, in glory great,
Fill the world with loud alarms,
　　And breathe a temporary hate :
The hoſtile ſtorms but rage awhile,
　　And the tir'd conteſt ends.
But ah ! how hard to reconcile
　　The foes who once were friends.

Each

Each hafty word, each look unkind,
 Each diftant hint, that feems to mean
A fomething lurking in the mind
 That almoft longs to lurk unfeen ;
Each fhadow of a fhade offends
Th' embittered foes who once were friends.

That Pow'r alone, who fram'd the Soul,
 And bade the fprings of paffion play,
Can all their jarring ftrings controul ;
 And form, on difcord, concord's fway.
'Tis He alone, whofe breath of love
Did o'er the world of waters move—
 Whofe touch the mountain bends—
Whofe word from darknefs call'd forth light ;
Tis He alone can reunite
 The foes who once were friends.

To Him, O Britain ! bow the knee.
His awful, his auguft decree,
 Ye rebel tribes adore !
Forgive at once and be forgiven :
Ope in each breaft a little heaven ;
 And difcord is no more !

A

A PASTORAL SONG.

[By Mr. STANSBURY, and purporting to have been written at Mr. Smith's in the Summer of 1778.]

WHEN War with its bellowing Sound
    Pervades each once happy retreat,
And Friendſhip no longer is found
    With thoſe who her praiſes repeat;
The good from the crowd may retire,
    And follow ſweet Peace to the Grove
Where Virtue rekindles her fire,
    And raiſes an altar to Love.

There bleſt with a ſociable few—
    The few that are juſt and ſincere—
We bid the ambitious adieu,
    And drop them, in pity, a tear,
We grieve at the fury and rage
    Which burn in the breaſts of our foes,
We fain would that fury aſſuage;
    We dare not that fury oppoſe.

With Peace and ſimplicity bleſt,
    No troubles our pleaſures annoy:
We quaff the pure ſtream with a zeſt
    The temp'rate alone can enjoy.
Thus innocent, chearful and gay
    The ſwift-fleeting moments ſecure:
An age would ſeem ſhort as a day
    With pleaſures as ſimple and pure.

A SONG FOR THE TIMES.

1778.

[By JOSEPH STANSBURY. This piece is a cloſe paraphraſe of *Plato's Advice* (Aikin on Song-writing, ed. 1810, p. 340), which itſelf was an alteration of the Rev. Matthew Pilkington's ſong, beginning, "Why, Lycidas, ſhould man be vain?" The alluſions are eaſily underſtood. In 1777, Congress had reſolved that the ſtars and ſtripes ſhould conſtitute our flag; and the treaty of alliance with France of February 6th, 1778, had inſpired the Whigs of America with the utmoſt gratitude and confidence.]

SAYS Cato, why ſhould Man be vain,
　Since bounteous Heav'n preſcribes his dates?
Or ſeek with ſo much fruitleſs pain
　　To form theſe independent States?
Can ſtriped Flags with Stars beſtrown,
　Or naked Wretches dragg'd to War,
Can upſtart Honors e'er atone
　　The pangs of Guilt or fierce Deſpair?

The Merchant's plan, the Farmer's toil,
　That raiſ'd our Wealth and Fame ſo high
And made our Plains like Britain's ſmile,
　　In Duſt without Diſtinction lie.
Go, ſearch for Gold the public Cheſt,
　Where once abundance heap'd her ſtore—
Our Wealth is Paper at the beſt;
　　And all its Credit is no more.

What tho' the Frenchman crowns the ſcene,
　And we miſcall him "Mankind's Friend;"
Not all his pow'r can Rebels ſcreen—
　　Rebellion's drawing near her end.

Shot

Shot like a Meteor thro' the Skies
   It ſpread awhile a baleful Train :
But now, by Jove's command it dies
   And melts to common Air again.

———

TO SIR JAMES WALLACE.

[Theſe verſes appear in Robertſon's Royal Pennſylvania Gazette, March 24th, 1778; and are there credited to a New York newspaper. Their author is ſaid to have been Dr. ODELL.[30]]

FYE! fye! Sir James! it cruel is
   Of the old Dutchman to make prize.
Tho', on enquiry, you may find
It was for good King Cong. deſigned,
Do'ſt think it is an honeſt job
This *Mity* bunch of Kings to rob ?[31]
The Wine they want to cheer their ſpirits :
The Cordage to reward their merits :
Tea's now no more a curſed plant;
It now has Virtue—which they want.
Their Linen and their Silks return—
They're all in rags; their garments torn!
Yet e'en of rags nigh deſtitute—
The bullion which their friends recruit.
Tho' by *Experiment*[32] you find
Their Bark is Jeſuits, reſcind :
And I dare tell you, free as wink,
Detain their *Salt*, they then muſt ſtink :
Or, if you mean at all to ſave,
Their Brandy let the Varlets have.[33]

THE CHURCH-AND-KING CLUB.

[Written by STANSBURY, apparently in the latter part of 1778, for a feftive meeting of a loyal affociation.34]

COME, honeft Tories, a truce with your Politics;
    Hoc age tells you in Latin as much :
Drink and be merry and—*à Melancholy, nix !*
    'Tis de fame ting do I fpeaks it in Dutch.
If old Diogenes lov'd altercation,
    Had he, fir, a drop of good Wine in his Tub ?
Mirth and Good-humour is *our* occupation :
    Let this be the Rule of the Church-and-King Club.

Well do we know the *Adelphi's* mifcarriages,
    And the difafters of Johnny Burgoyne ;
As to Beef-Stakes, no good fellow difparages
    One who in *battle* finds *leifure to dine.*35

Congo pretends (O good Lord, what a Fibber 'tis !)
    Now to *feel bold*, and to fear no mifchance.
As well might he fay that he fights *for their liberties*,
    Whom he hath fold in a *mortgage* to France !36

Soon fhall you fee *a rebellious minority*
    Blufh for the part they have acted fo long ;
Britain fhall roufe and regain her authority :
    Come then, a Bumper, and call t'other Song.
If old Diogenes lov'd altercation, &c.

                        CHURCH

CHURCH AND KING.

[Written by JOSEPH STANSBURY *circa* January, 1779.]

IN days of yore when, free and unconfin'd,
    Man rov'd at large, and his own Will was law,
No ties reſtrain'd his ſelfiſh ſavage Mind;
The Mighty kept the Weak in ſlaviſh awe.
Till ſome ſagacious Soul, pervading thro' the whole,
    To Harmony reduc'd each jarring ſtring;
And now the tuneful Band obeys the Maſter's hand,
    While Echo ſounds reſponſive Church and King!

In theſe, our vain and motley modern times,
When Whim, not Reaſon blindly leads the way;
And Virtue's varniſh covers o'er our crimes,
Abhorrent to the honeſt face of Day;
Now Freedom ſtrikes the Lyre, and vainly would inſpire
Celeſtial Ardor to each broken String:
But we deſpiſe the Foe, and by Experience know
    No Harmony's compleat without Church and King.

Tho' Rage vindictive Meaſures would inſpire,
And hurl promiscuous Ruin far and wide;
Yet Mercy checks the Britiſh Hero's fire
And Pity gently pours her ſoftening tide.
By Fate's ſupreme Decree this happy Year ſhall ſee
    The Royal Standard ev'ry Straggler bring,
Like Sheep, into the Fold from which they thoughtleſs ſtroll'd,
    To join in laſting Chorus of Church and King.

                                              Then

Then, let each firm and trufty loyalHeart
Relate with glee his tale of fuff'ring o'er;
And think with pride, he bravely play'd his part
And reach'd triumphant the long wifh'd for fhore.
The wreath let Victory twine, immortal and divine;
    The Laurel and the Bay let Fame now bring:
While Time fhall hobble round, all Pleafures fhall
        abound,
    And the Virtues and Graces crown Church and King.

———

TO PEACE.

[From the Manufcripts of Joseph Stansbury.]

O COME, light borne on eaftern gales,
    And bid our forrows ceafe:
With flow'rets crown our fmiling Vales
Thou gentle Cherub Peace!
Efface the horrid marks of War;
Each private Grudge remove;
With Plenty load the ruftic's Car,
And fill the Land with Love.

THE TOWN MEETING.

[This clever but bitter piece was written by JOSEPH STANSBURY, and firſt publiſhed at New York in Rivington's Royal Gazette, No. 286 ; June 26th, 1779 : under the title of *An Hiſtorical Ballad of the Proceedings at Philadelphia,* 24th and 25th May, 1779, *by a Loyaliſt who happened to paſs through the City at that Time, on his way from the Southward to New York.* It is here printed from the text in Rivington, collated with ſeveral contemporaneous manuſcript copies.[37]]

CANTO FIRST.

'TWAS on the twenty-fourth of May,
    A pleaſant, warm, ſun-ſhiny day,
      Militia folks paraded
With colours ſpread, with cannon too ;
Such loud huzzas, ſuch martial ſhew ;
      I thought the town invaded !

But when, on cloſer look, I ſpied
The *Speaker* march with gallant ſtride,
      I knew myſelf miſtaken :
For he, on Trenton's well-fought day,
To Burlington *miſtook* his way,
      And fairly ſav'd his bacon.[38]

With him a number more appear'd
Whoſe names their Corporals never heard —
      To muſter-rolls a ſtranger :
To ſave their fines they took the Gun ;
Determined with the firſt to run
      On any glimpſe of danger,

The

The great *M'Clenǫchan* beſtrode
His prancing horſe, and fiercely rode :
          And faith, he had good reaſon !
For he was told that, to his ſorrow,
He, with a number more, tomorrow
          Should be confin'd in priſon.[39]

'Tis ſaid, ſome ſpeculating job
Of his had ſo inflam'd the mob
          That they were grown unruly ;
And, ſwearing "by the Eternal God "
Such villains now ſhould feel the rod,
          Reſolv'd to "come on coolly."

The People's Majeſty—of Laws
The proper end, the only cauſe—
          Now ſhone in all its glory ![40]
—*Morris* the wife ; *Arnold* the brave ;
The double *Maſon* ; *Wiſtar* grave—
          Confounded with the Tory ![41]

Nor age, nor wealth, nor rank, nor birth
Avail'd with theſe true ſons of earth,
          The offſpring of the Valley :
For all the lore of ages paſt
What car'd the Stateſman with his Laſt,[42]
          Or Hero of the Alley ?

Cover'd with ſweat, with bawling hoarſe,
At cloſe of day no tired horſe
          More gladly reach'd his home.
Each doft his oaken civic crown :[43]
Firſt took a dram—then laid him down
          And dream'd of joys to come.

CANTO

CANTO SECOND.

Now Titan raiſ'd his flaming head,
And drowſy Centinels to bed
      Retir'd from irkſome duty:
For they were plac'd, as it behov'd,
To watch if Tory Goods were mov'd,
      That they might ſhare the booty.

The Mob tumultuous inſtant ſeize
With venom'd rage on whom they pleaſe;
      The People cannot err!
Can it be wrong, in Freedom's cauſe,
To tread down juſtice, order, laws,
      When all the mob concur?

But now, thro' *Mitchell's* brazen throat,
Faction with loud, abuſive note
      Proclaim'd a *Grand Town* Meeting:
Where printer's devils, barber's boys,[44]
Apprentice lads, expreſs their joys
      The Council Members greeting.

Each vagabond from whipping poſt,[45]
Or ſtranger ſtranded on the coaſt,[46]
      May here reform the State:
The Porter *Will*,[47] and *Shad-roe Jack*,[48]
And Pompey-like *McKean*, in black,[49]
      Decide a People's fate.

The Trained Bands of Germantown
With Clubs and Bayonets came down,
      And ſwell'd the motley train;
Reſolv'd to change, like him of old,
Old rags and lampblack[50] into Gold,
      Or Chaos bring again.

And

And now the State-houfe yard was full,
And Orators fo grave, fo dull,
  Appear'd upon the ftage :
But all was riot, noife, difgrace;
And Freedom's fons thro' all the place
  In bloody frays engage.

Sagacious *Matlack*[51] ftrove in vain
To pour his fenfe in Dutchmen's brain,
  With ev'ry art to pleafe :
Obferv'd "that as their Money fell.
" Like Lucifer, to loweft Hell,
  " Tho' fwift, yet by degrees —

" So fhould it rife, and goods fhould fall
" Month after month, and one and all
  " Would buy as cheap as ever ;
" That they loft all, who grafp'd too much"—
(This Colonel *Bull*[52] explain'd in Dutch),
  —But fruitlefs each endeavour.

With folemn phiz and action flow,
Arofe the Chairman, *Roberdeau*,[53]
  And made this humane motion:
' That Tories, with their brats and wives,
Should fly, to fave their wretched lives,
  From Sodom into—Gofhen.'[54]

He central ftood, and all the ground
With people cover'd, him furround;
  And thence it came to pafs
That, as he fpoke with zeal upon't,
He turn'd his face to thofe in front;
  To thofe behind, ———

        This

This gave offence—his voice was drown'd.
He ſhould have ſhown his face all round,
  Like whirligig in ſocket:
Or, if that did his art ſurpaſs,
He ſhould at leaſt have ta'en ————
  And put it in his pocket.[55]

Then *Hutchinſon*,[56] that great bull-calf—
A gander has more brains by half—[57]
  In croaking, froglike note
Approv'd the motion, and demands
The People's ſenſe, by ſhew of hands,
  To ſave or damn the vote.

All raiſ'd their hands, with mighty burſt
Of loud acclaim—The caſe reverſ'd,
  All lift their hands again!
Blue *Bayard* grinn'd—that long-ear'd aſs—
With mobs he ſaw it was a farce
  To reaſon or explain.

But thoughtful *Ruſh*,[58] and artful *Gaff*,[59]
And *Bryan*,[60] too much vex'd to laugh,
  Were fill'd with grief and pity ;
And ſoon diſmiſſ'd the Rabble Rout:
Concluding what they were about
  With chuſing a Committee.

Hoping to get them more in tune
Before the twenty-fifth of June,
  Which was the choſen day
For them to meet by ſound of Drum ;
Unleſs the Enemy ſhould come
  And make them run away.

        To

To tell their Tale, away they ſpeed
To their *prime mover, Joſeph Reed,*
  " *The virtuous and ſublime!* "
So *virtuous,* that he cheats his friends,
Sublimely cheats to gain his ends;
  And glories in the crime.

Ambition is his darling theme:
Integrity an idle dream
  That vulgar minds may awe.
At home, abroad, with friend or wife,
In public or in private life,
  The tyrant's will is law.

Of deep reſentments, wicked, bold,
The thirſt of Blood, of Power, of Gold,
  Poſſeſs alternate ſway:
And *Johnſtone's* bribe had ſurely won
Rebellion's pale-fac'd matchleſs ſon,
  Had *Mammon* rul'd that day.[61]

But time would fail me to rehearſe
In my poor limping doggrel verſe,
  His character divine:
Suffice it that in *Dunlap's* page,
Drawn by himſelf, from age to age
  It ſhall with ſplendor ſhine![62]

THE CONGRATULATION.

𝔄 𝔓oem.

Dii boni, boni quid porto.—TERENCE.

[Written by Rev. Dr. ODELL, on occaſion of the failure of the great expeᔑations entertained by the Americans from the preſence in our waters of D'Eſtaing's fleet during the years 1778 and 1779. This piece appears to have been very popular at the period, being printed at New York in Rivington's Royal Gazette of November 6th, 1779; and again in the Supplement of November 24th.[63]]

JOY to great Congreſs, joy an hundred fold :
  The grand cajolers are themſelves cajol'd !
In vain has [Franklin's] artifice been tried,
And Louis ſwell'd with treachery and pride :
Who reigns ſupreme in heav'n deception ſpurns,
And on the author's head the miſchief turns.
What pains were taken to procure D'Eſtaing !
His fleet's diſperſ'd, and Congreſs may go hang.

Joy to great Congreſs, joy an hundred fold :
The grand cajolers are themſelves cajol'd !
Heav'ns King ſends forth the hurricane and ſtrips
Of all their glory the perfidious ſhips.
His Miniſters of Wrath the ſtorm direᔑ ;
Nor can the Prince of Air his French proteᔑ.
Saint George, Saint David ſhow'd themſelves true
    hearts ;
Saint Andrew and Saint Patrick topp'd their parts.
With right Eolian puffs the wind they blew ;
Crack went the maſts ; the ſails to ſhivers flew.
Such honeſt Saints ſhall never be forgot ;
Saint Dennis, and Saint Tammany, go rot.[64]

Joy

Joy to great Congreſs, joy an hundred fold;
The grand cajolers are themſelves cajol'd!
Old Satan holds a council in mid-air;
Hear the black Dragon furious rage and ſwear—
—Are theſe the triumphs of my Gallic friends?
How will you ward this blow, my truſty fiends?
What remedy for this unlucky job?
What art ſhall raiſe the ſpirits of the mob?
Fly ſwift, ye ſure ſupporters of my realm,
Ere this ill-news the rebels overwhelm.
Invent, ſay any thing to make them mad;
Tell them the King—No, Dev'ls are not ſo bad;
The dogs of Congreſs at the King let looſe;
But ye, brave Dev'ls, avoid ſuch mean abuſe.

Joy to great Congreſs, joy an hundred fold:
The grand cajolers are themſelves cajol'd!
What thinks Sir Waſhington of this miſchance;
Blames he not thoſe, who put their truſt in France?
A broken reed comes pat into his mind:
Egypt and France by ruſhes are defin'd,
Baſeſt of Kingdoms underneath the ſkies,
Kingdoms that could not profit their allies.
How could the tempeſt play him ſuch a prank?
Blank is his proſpect, and his viſage blank:
Why from Weſt-Point his armies has he brought?
Can nought be done?—ſore ſighs he at the thought.
Back to his mountains Waſhington may trot:
He take this city—yes, when Ice is hot.

Joy to great Congreſs, joy an hundred fold:
The grand cajolers are themſelves cajol'd!
Ah, poor militia of the Jerſey State,
Your hopes are bootleſs, you are come too late.
                                    Your

Your four hours plunder of New-York is fled,
And grievous hunger haunts you in its ſtead.
Sorrow and ſighing ſeize the Yankee race,
When the brave Briton looks them in the face:
The brawny Heſſian, the bold Refugee,
Appear in arms, and lo ! the rebels flee;
Each in his bowels griping *ſpankue* feels;
Each drops his haverſack, and truſts his heels.
Scamp'ring and ſcouring o'er the fields they run,
And here you find a ſword, and there a gun.

Joy to great Congreſs, joy an hundred fold ;
The grand cajolers are themſelves cajol'd !
The doleful tidings Philadelphia reach,
And Duffield[65] cries—The wicked make a breach !
Members of Congreſs in confuſion meet,
And with pale countenance each other greet.
—No comfort, brother ?—Brother, none at all.
Fall'n is our tower ; yea, broken down our wall.
Oh brother ! things are at a dreadful paſs :
Brother, we ſinn'd in going to the Maſs.
The Lord, who taught our fingers how to fight,
For this denied to curb the tempeſt's might :
Our paper coin refuſ'd for flour we ſee,
And lawyers will not take it for a fee.

Joy to great Congreſs, joy an hundred fold :
The grand cajolers are themſelves cajol'd !
What cauſ'd the French from Parker's fleet to ſteal ?
They wanted thirty thouſand caſks of meal.
Where are they now—can mortal man reply ?
Who finds them out muſt have a Lynx's eye.
Some place them in the ports of Cheſapeak ;
Others account them bound to Martinique ;

Some

Some think to Boſton they intend to go ;
And ſome ſuppoſe them in the deep below.
One thing is certain, be they where they will,
They keep their triumph moſt exceeding ſtill.
They have not even Pantagruel's luck,
Who conquer'd two old women and a duck.[66]

Joy to great Congreſs, joy an hundred fold :
The grand cajolers are themſelves cajol'd !
How long ſhall the deluded people look
For the French ſquadron moor'd at Sandy Hook ?
Of all their hopes the comfort and the ſtay,
This vile deceit at length muſt paſs away.
What impoſition can be thought on next,
To cheer their partizans, with doubt perplex'd ?
Dollars on dollars heap'd up to the ſkies,
Their value ſinks the more, the more they riſe ;
Bank notes of bankrupts, ſtruck without a fund,
Puff'd for a ſeaſon, will at laſt be ſhunn'd.
Call forth invention, ye renown'd in guile ;
New falſehoods frame in matter, and in ſtyle ;
Send ſome enormous fiction to the preſs ;
Again prepare the circular addreſs ;
With lies, with nonſenſe, keep the people drunk :
For ſhould they once reflect, your power is ſunk,

Joy to great Congreſs, joy an hundred fold :
The grand cajolers are themſelves cajol'd !
The farce of empire will be finiſh'd ſoon,
And each mock-monarch dwindle to a loon.
Mock-money and mock-ſtates ſhall melt away,
And the mock-troops diſband for want of pay.
Ev'n now deciſive ruin is prepar'd :
Ev'n now the heart of Huntington is ſcar'd.[67]

Seen

Seen or unſeen, on earth, above, below,
All things conſpire to give the final blow.
Heaven has ten thouſand thunderbolts to dart ;
From Hell, ten thouſand livid flames will ſtart ;
Myriads of ſwords are ready for the field ;
Myriads of lurking daggers are conceal'd ;
In injur'd boſoms dark revenge is nurſt :
Yet but a moment, and the ſtorm ſhall burſt.

Joy to great Congreſs, joy an hundred fold :
The grand cajolers are themſelves cajol'd !
Now War, ſuſpended by the ſcorching heat,
Springs from his tent, and ſhines in arms complete.
Now Sickneſs, that of late made heroes pale,
Flies from the keenneſs of the northern gale.
Firmneſs and Enterprize, united, wait
The laſt command, to ſtrike the ſtroke of Fate.
Now Boſton trembles ; Philadelphia quakes ;
And Carolina to the center ſhakes.
There is, whoſe councils the juſt moment ſcan :
Whoſe wiſdom meditates the mighty plan :
He, when the ſeaſon is mature, ſhall ſpeak ;
All Heaven ſhall plaud him, and all Hell ſhall ſhriek.
At his dread fiat tumult ſhall retire ;
Abhorr'd rebellion ſicken and expire ;
The fall of Congreſs prove the world's relief ;
And deathleſs glory crown the god-like Chief !

Joy to great Congreſs, joy an hundred fold :
The grand cajolers are themſelves cajol'd !
What now is left of Continental brags ?
Taxes unpaid, tho' payable in rags.
What now remains of Continental force ?
Battalions mould'ring : Waſte without reſource.

What

What reſts there yet of Continental Sway?
A ruin'd People, ripe to diſobey.
Hate now of men, and ſoon to be the Jeſt;
Such is your fate, ye Monſters of the Weſt!
Yet muſt on every face a ſmile be worn,
While every breaſt with agony is torn.
Hopeleſs yourſelves, yet hope you muſt impart,
And comfort others with an aching heart.
Ill-fated they who, loſt at home, muſt boaſt
Of help expeᴄted from a foreign coaſt:
How wretched is their lot, to France and Spain
Who look for ſuccour, but who look in vain.

Joy to great Congreſs, joy an hundred fold:
The grand cajolers are themſelves cajol'd!
Courage, my boys; diſmiſs your chilling fears:
Attend to me, I'll put you in your geers.
Come, I'll inſtruᴄt you how to advertize
Your miſſing friends, your hide-and-ſeek Allies.
O YES!—If any man alive will bring
News of the ſquadron of the Chriſtian King:
If any man will find out Count D'Eſtaing,
With whoſe ſcrub aᴄtions both the Indies rang:
If any man will aſcertain on oath
What has become of Monſieur de la Mothe:[68]
Whoever theſe important points explains,
Congreſs will nobly pay him for his pains,
Of pewter dollars, what both hands can hold,
A thimble-full of plate, a mite of gold;
The lands of ſome big Tory he ſhall get,
And ſtart a famous Colonel *en brevet:*
And laſt to honour him (we ſcorn to bribe)
We'll make him chief of the *Oneida* Tribe![69]

THE

THE FEU DE JOIE.

𝔄 𝔓oem.

Urgetur pugna Congreſſus iniqua.—VIRGIL.

[Written by the REV. DR. ODELL, and printed here from
Rivington's Royal Gazette of November 24th, 1779. The
gallant and ſucceſſful defence of Savannah by the Britiſh under
Prevoſt, Maitland, and Moncrieffe, and the final repulſe of the
Allies led by Lincoln and D'Eſtaing, on the 9th of October, 1779,
occaſioned great exultation in the Britiſh army at New York,
and gave origin to theſe verſes. Their title relates to the cuſtom
of celebrating any victory or other occaſion of triumph in the
American (and perhaps in the Britiſh) Army, by a general diſcharge of firearms.]

LET ſongs of triumph every voice employ,
  And every Muſe diſcharge a *feu de joie!*
Hail, Congreſs, hail! magnificent, renown'd:
Rejoice, be merry; the loſt Sheep is found!
You, Congreſs, knew him by his graceful bleat.
We only know him by his foul defeat.
Great Bell Wether, he led his ſcabby flock
In apt conjunction with the rebel ſtock.
He came, he puſh'd, he fled with half his train;
While ſav'd Savannah ſwell'd with heaps of ſlain.

Let ſongs of triumph every voice employ,
And every Muſe diſcharge a feu de joie!
What awful ſilence thro' the land prevail'd
Since Count D'Eſtaing from St. Domingo ſail'd.
No voice, no breath, no ſound, no rumour flew,
Leſt Parker ſhould with all his fleet purſue.[70]

No

No whifper; no report—but all was mum,
Left reinforcements from New York fhould come.
To catch the Britifh napping was their thought:
Now, by my faith, a Tartar have they caught.

Let fongs of triumph every voice employ,
And every Mufe difcharge a feu de joie!
The French, entangled in a dreadful fcrape,
From the Weft-Indies made a fine efcape.
Arriv'd upon the coaft, the fcene was chang'd:
Uncivil Winds their armament derang'd;
Their firft reception was exceeding rough;
Howe'er they landed: landed fure enough.
Afhore, they vapour and defy the Storm,
And foon with *Lincoln's* troops a junction form.

Let fongs of triumph every voice employ,
And every Mufe difcharge a feu de joie!
Plunder's the Word; but Plunder foon is o'er.
Rob folks of all, and you can rob no more.
Live ftock or dead, they capture and condemn:
Come Whig, come Tory, 'tis the fame to them.
The Continental gentry ftand aghaft
To fee their good Allies devour fo faft.
Are thefe the Troops of Louis, Friend of Men?
They're rather Tygers, loofen'd from a Den.

Let fongs of triumph every voice employ,
And every Mufe difcharge a feu de joie!
The fworn confederates manfully advance
In queft of Glory and the Good of France.
Go fummon, Trumpeter, yon haughty Town:
Bid them furrender to the Gallic Crown.[71]
What, are they reftiff?—fcorn they to obey?
Pefte—we'll compel them with what fpeed we may.

Erect

Erect your batteries, Engineers, in haſte:
Mortars and Cannons in the Works be plac'd.
Upon the right my valiant French ſhall load;
You Continentals, line th' Auguſta road.
Moncrieffe ſeems active, but he'll ſoon be ſick,
When ſhells and balls and bullets rattle thick.[72]

Let ſongs of triumph every voice employ,
And every Muſe diſcharge a feu de joie!
The brave D'Eſtaing encourages his troops,
And promiſes good ſtore of drams and ſoups.
Work on, work on, ye jolly Pioneers.
The town ſhall ſoon be knock'd about their ears.
Meantime, ſtrict guard about the camp we'll keep,
And neither in nor out a mouſe ſhall creep.
But whence ariſes, in the dead of night,
This horrid noiſe to fill us with affright?
Are all the devils got looſe?—D'Eſtaing cries out.
—No, ſir, 'tis Maitland puts us to the rout.[73]
Stop him this inſtant!—Sir, he won't be ſtopt.
Chop him—*En verite*, ourſelves are chopt.
The town he ſhall not enter, I declare,
—True, noble Count, for he's already there.

Let ſongs of triumph every voice employ,
And every Muſe diſcharge a feu de joie!
The Gallic Chief, his batteries complete,
Conceives the Britiſh humbled at his feet.
Full thirty cannons, mortars half a ſcore;
No doubt Prevoſt muſt tremble at their roar.
They open, and proclaim Savannah's doom;
Hide day with ſmoke, with flaſhes night illume.
Now whiſtle through the air the pond'rous plumbs;
Now mount aloft, and now deſcend the bombs.
Inceſſant thunders rend the frighted ſky,
And bluffs and hillocks to the ſound reply.

Let

Let fongs of triumph every voice employ,
And every Mufe difcharge a feu de joie !
What great effect has all this fire produc'd ?
Here falls an houfe, and there a turf is loof'd.
What, no flain warriors tumbled in the trench ?
Yes, by the Mafs :—abundance of the French !
No cannon yet difmounted can you fee ?
Oh yes—a number marked with *Fleurs de Lys.*
Where are the Yankees ?—where they were at firft.
What have we got then ?—we have got the worft.
How can this be ?   Six days, and nothing done !
The cafe is plain—the foe gives three for one.
Our thirty cannon have no chance at all,
Moncrieffe falutes with ninety from the wall.
Pize on't—this way of fiege is moft abfurd :
We'll have no more on't—Storm fhall be the word !

Let fongs of triumph every voice employ,
And every Mufe difcharge a feu de joie !
The Veterans of France have form'd the line,
Expecting daybreak and the promif'd fign.
The Rebel Bands are marfhall'd in array,
Boaftful and loud, and covetous of prey.
What held the Town of beauty, wealth, and power,
Was all devoted in that cruel hour.
Sore figh'd the Mother, for her Babes afraid ;
And, anxious for herfelf, the blooming Maid.
The Merchant trembled for his crouded ftore :
One dreadful paufe—and all perhaps is gore !
So to the rock Andromeda lay bound,
When rofe the Monfter from the vaft profound :
But foon her brave Deliverer fac'd the foe ;
No matter whether *Perfeus* or *Prevoft.*
His winged courfer gallant he beftrode ;
He look'd a Hero, and he mov'd a God !

He

He met the Monſter in his fierce attack,
And to old Ocean headlong drove him back.

Let ſongs of triumph every voice employ,
And every Muſe diſcharge a feu de joie!
Lo! from the Artillery pours the grand ſalute:
Then Silence flows—and all is huſh'd and mute.
Sudden the drum rebellows; ſwells the fife;
And all move forward to the mortal ſtrife.
The ſhouting warriors and the trumpets ſhrill
The meaneſt heart with martial ardour fill.
With rapid march advance the hoſtile rows,
While Britiſh fire the ranks tremendous mows.
Now nearer ſtill and nearer they engage,
And War puts on accumulated rage.
There is the din of battle; there the craſh;
The roaring volley, and the frequent flaſh.
There animation in the front appears:
There charge the choſen Gallic Grenadiers.
There, where each moment death they take or give,
Scarce Immortality herſelf could live!

Let ſongs of triumph every voice employ,
And every Muſe diſcharge a feu de joie!
Now Slaughter triumphed and refiſtleſs ſtrow'd
With mangled carcaſſes the reeking road.
Ev'n then, when blood was ſtreaming like a fount,
Polaſki ruſh'd the ſtrong Redoubt to mount.
Again the grape-ſhot thunders from the walls:
He falls—half hero, half a fiend, he falls.
Off from the field his ſoldiers bear their chief;
Art was invok'd, but Art gave no relief;
Deep in his groin was fix'd the deadly wound.
Worthleſs, tho' brave, a glorious fate he found.

Such

Such noble death what right had he to hope,
Whoſe odius Treaſon merited a Rope?
Undaunted minds were made in verſe to ſhine?
But hate to parricides blots out the line.
Not Valour's ſelf the Traitor can excuſe:
Him Truth condemns: him execrates the Muſe.[74]

Let ſongs of triumph every voice employ,
And every Muſe diſcharge a feu de joie!
Such deſperate efforts the battalions thin.
Diſorder and diſmay and rout begin.
The worn brigades from fight recoiling ſwerve;
Their courage droops, they faint in every nerve.
Yet ſtill remains an excellent reſource—
Bring to the charge the Continental Force.
What ails theſe Braggadocios of the Land?
Won't they come forward?—ſtiff as Poſts they ſtand.
Strange petrifaction on their hoſt attends.
Deuce take the fools, they level at their friends!
Some angry Demon ſure their ſenſe miſleads;
See, the French tremble, and their General bleeds,
By rebel hands (Lo! Providence is juſt)
The rebels' patron wounded bites the duſt.[75]

Let ſongs of triumph every voice employ,
And every Muſe diſcharge a feu de joie!
'Tis done: Confuſion ſits on every face;
Inevitable ruin; foul diſgrace.
Now Terror domineers, and wild Affright:
No hope in Arms: no ſafety but in Flight.
Now, Britons, Heſſians and Provincials pour:
Arreſt the fugitives and bathe in gore.
'Tis done:—D'Eſtaing betakes him to his ſhip;
To Charleſtown Yankies thro' the foreſts ſlip.

Go

Go reckon up thy loſs, amphibious Count;
Mark Fifteen Hundred to the full amount:
Of wounded and of killed an equal train
Left Lincoln weltering on the bloody plain:
Whilſt forty Britons on the liſt appear.
O Earth confeſs, the Hand of Heaven was here!

Let ſongs of triumph every voice employ,
And every Muſe diſcharge a feu de joie!
Does Lordly Congreſs reliſh this defeat—
Say, is it pleaſant to their ſouls and ſweet?
What, both o'erthrown, America and France,
By one ſmall ſplinter of the Britiſh Lance!
Yet theſe were they, gigantic in their boaſt,
Who ſwore to chaſe us from this Weſtern Coaſt:
Yet theſe were they who built flat-bottomed boats,
And vow'd to drive us like a Flock of Goats.
Unſtable as the ſand, their arts ſhall fail:
As water weak, they never ſhall prevail.
Theſe, Reuben-like, their parent's couch defile;
Like Judas, theſe ſhall periſh in their guile.
Could the Sword ſpare them, yet of Heaven accurſt
Their very Bowels would aſunder burſt.

Let ſongs of triumph every voice employ,
And every Muſe diſcharge a feu de joie!
Ye poor deluded owners of the ſoil,
For others' good who labour and who toil —
Ye wretches doom'd to ſorrowful miſtake,
Who hunger and who thirſt for Congreſs' ſake—
Arouſe for Shame: like Men your rights reſume,
And ſend your Tyrants to the Land of Gloom.
If Shame prevail not, ſtill let Wiſdom plead.
If both are ſlighted, Vengeance muſt ſucceed.

Your

Your Parent State grows ſtronger every hour;
As yet, its Mercy far exceeds its Power.
Your Congreſs every moment weaker grows.
Rags are its Treaſure: Honeſt Men its Foes.
Its Building cracks, tho' buttreſſ'd by the Gaul:
It nods, it ſhakes, it totters to its fall.
O ſave yourſelves before it is too late!
O ſave your Country from impending Fate!
Leave thoſe, whom Juſtice muſt at length deſtroy.
Repent, come over, and partake our joy.

ODE FOR THE NEW YEAR.

[Written at New York, January 1ſt, 1780, by Dr. ODELL,
and now printed from his Manuſcript copy.]

WHEN rival Nations firſt deſcried,
    Emerging from the boundleſs Main
This Land by Tyrants yet untried,
On high was ſung this lofty ſtrain:
Riſe Britannia beaming far!
Riſe bright Freedom's morning ſtar!

To diſtant Regions unexplor'd
Extend the bleſſings of thy ſway;
To yon benighted World afford
The light of thy all-chearing ray;
Riſe Britannia, riſe bright ſtar!
Spread thy radiance wide and far!

The

The ſhoots of Science rich and fair,
Tranſplanted from thy foſtering Iſle
And by thy Genius nurtur'd there,
Shall teach the Wildernefs to ſmile.
Shine, Britannia, rife and ſhine!
To blefs Mankind the taſk be thine!

Nor ſhall the Mufes now difdain
To find a new Aſylum there:
And ripe for harveſt fee the plain,
Where lately rov'd the prowling Bear.
Plume, Britannia, plume thy wing!
Teach the favage Wild to fing!

From thee defcended, there the Swain
Shall arm the Port and fpread the Sail,
And fpeed his traffick o'er the Main
With ſkill to brave the fweeping Gale;
Skill, Britannia, taught by thee,
Unrivall'd Emprefs of the Sea!

This high and holy ſtrain how true
Had now from age to age been ſhown;
And to the World's admiring view
Rofe Freedom's tranfatlantic throne:
Here, Britannia, here thy fame
Long did we with joy proclaim.

But ah! what frenzy breaks a band
Of love and union held fo dear!
Rebellion madly ſhakes the land,
And love is turn'd to hate and fear.
Here, Britannia, here at laſt
We feel Contagion's deadly blaſt.

Thus

Thus blind, alas ! when all is well,
Thus blind are Mortals here below :
As when apoſtate Angels fell,
Ambition turns our blifs to woe.
Now, Britannia, now beware :
For other conflicts now prepare !

By thee controul'd for ages paſt,
See now half Europe in array :
For wild Ambition hopes at laſt
To fix her long projected ſway.
Riſe, Britannia, riſe again
The ſcourge of haughty France and Spain !

The howling tempeſt fiercely blows,
And Ocean rages in the ſtorm :
'Tis then the fearleſs Pilot ſhows
What Britiſh courage can perform.
Rule, Britannia, rule the waves
And ruin all intruding ſlaves !

THE

THE LORDS OF THE MAIN.

Tune: *Nottingham Ale.*

[Publifhed at New York, February 16th, 1780, in Rivington's
Royal Gazette, and believed to have been written by STANSBURY.
In this, as in the piece immediately preceding, reference is made
to the hoftilities between Spain and England which had broken
out in the paft fummer.   The other allufions to Carpenter's Hall
at Philadelphia, where Congrefs met ; to Congrefs itfelf, and to
the French Alliance, will be readily underftood.   The tenth line
of the laft Stanza feems to have been a favorite : it is already
ufed by the poet in an earlier page of this volume.]

WHEN Faction, in league with the treacherous
   Gaul,
 Began to look big and paraded in ftate ;
A meeting was held at *Credulity Hall*,
 And Echo proclaim'd their Ally *good and great* !
   By fea and by land
   Such wonders are plann'd ;
No lefs than the bold Britifh Lion to chain !
   Well hove ! fays *Jack Lanyard*,
   French, Congo and Spaniard,
Have at you—remember we're Lords of the Main !
 Lords of the Main—aye, Lords of the Main ;
The Tars of Old England are Lords of the Main.

Though party-contention a while may perplex,
 And lenity hold us in doubtful fufpenfe ;
If perfidy roufe, or ingratitude vex
 In defiance of Hell we'll chaftife the offence.
   When danger alarms,
   'Tis then that in arms
        United

United we ruſh on the foe with diſdain :
    And when the ſtorm rages
    It only preſages
Freſh triumphs to Britons, as Lords of the Main.
   Lords of the Main—ay, Lords of the Main—
Let *Thunder* proclaim it, we're Lords of the Main.

Then Britons, *ſtrike home*—make ſure of your blow :
   The chaſe is in view ; never mind a lee-ſhoṛe.
With vengeance o'ertake the confederate foe :
   'Tis now we may rival our heroes of yore !
    Brave *Anſon* and *Drake*,
    Hawke, *Ruſſell* and *Blake*,
With ardour like your's we defy France and Spain !
    Combining with *Treaſon*
    They're deaf to all reaſon :
Once more let them *feel* we are Lords of the Main.
   Lords of the Main—ay, Lords of the Main—
The firſt-born of Neptune are Lords of the Main.

Nor are we alone in the noble career ;
   The *Soldier* partakes of the generous flame :
To glory he marches, to glory we ſteer ;
   Between us we ſhare the rich harveſt of fame.
    Recorded on high,
    Their names never die,
Of heroes by ſea and by land what a train !
    To the *King*, then, God bleſs him !
    The *World* ſhall confeſs him
' The Lord of thoſe men who are Lords of the Main.'
   Lords of the Main—ay, Lords of the Main—
The Tars of Old England are Lords of the Main.

                     LIBERTY.

LIBERTY.

[" The following piece " ſays Rivington's Royal Gazette, No. 352, February 12th, 1780, " is ſuppoſed to be written by a Loyaliſt without the lines." There is ſatiſfactory evidence, how-ever, that Mr. STANSBURY was its author.]

WHEN at firſt this land I preſt,
  'Pleaſing rapture fill'd my breaſt;
Swains in carols ſweet and free
Sung the praiſe of Liberty.
Now their Halcyon days are o'er;
Fled to ſome more happy ſhore.
There, from civil Diſcord free
Dwells the Goddeſs Liberty.

At Bellona's harſh alarms
Simple yeomen ſhine in arms.
Brother ſlain by brother, ſee !
Dreadful fruits of Liberty.
Law and order proſtrate lie ;
Commonwealth is all the cry.
Tho' we ſlaves at preſent be
'Tis all for glorious Liberty.

What tho' Commerce droops her head,
All her ſons to deſerts fled :
Let's to *Clinton* bow the knee ;
We're ſecure of Liberty.
Wealth propitious ſwells our ſtore ;
All our Coffers running o'er ;
Dollars cheap as dirt ſhall be.
Who wou'd not fight for Liberty ?

                                        Splendid

Splendid honours I diſdain:
Crowns of Kings are lin'd with Pain.
Friendſhip only give to me,
Social joys, and Liberty.
Let me in my humble ſphere
Free from envy, free from care,
Spend the days allotted me
Bleſt with Peace and Liberty.

———

FREEDOM.

[Collated from two verſions in the Manuſcripts of Mr. STANS-
BURY, and dated March 5th, 1780. It is hardly neceſſary to add
that the ſong is ironical.]

TO Freedom raiſe the lofty ſong.
   Sublimeſt joys to her belong.
'Tis ſhe that ſmooths the face of War;
Hides with laurel ev'ry ſcar.
Huzza for the bleſſings of Freedom, oh!

To her we owe, that fix'd as fate
Appears our independent State;
Our crowded ports and growing trade;
Honours too, which ne'er ſhall fade.
Theſe, theſe are the bleſſings of Freedom, oh!

'Tis She produc'd thoſe wiſe and great
And honeſt men who rule the State;
To meaner trades no more confined—
Awls and handſaws left behind—
How great are the bleſſings of Freedom, oh!

Some

Some wretches may diſgrace the Cauſe
(For human nature's full of flaws)
And filch away the public wealth :
Speculate—by way of ſtealth—
Diſgracing the banners of Freedom, oh !

The Tories cry our Paper down ;
Count forty dollars but a crown :
For which we'll tax and plague them more
Than Pharaoh's ſlaves in days of yore ;
And all for the honour of Freedom, oh !

Then fill the glaſs to Fredom, oh !
Fill up the glaſs to Freedom, oh !
May the preſent conteſt hold
Till my Paper's turn'd to Gold—
Then, a fig for the battle for Freedom, oh !

On

ON ADMIRAL ARBUTHNOT.

A PASQUINADE STUCK UP AT NEW YORK, AUGUST 12TH,
1780.

[This piece is attributed to Mr. STANSBURY, and is a fair
example of the manner in which the inertneſs of the Engliſh
leaders was criticized by the loyaliſts. It is preſerved in the
Political Magazine, vol. II, p. 291 (London, May, 1781). It
refers to the failure of Sir Henry Clinton's plan of an attack on
the French fleet and troops lately arrived at Rhode Iſland by a
co-operation of the Britiſh land and naval forces from New
York. [76]]

OF Arbuthnot, my friend, pray tell me the news;
What's done by his ſhips and their brave gallant
crews?
Has the old Engliſh man ſhewn old Engliſh ſpunk
And the ſhips of the French burnt, taken, or ſunk?

In truth, my good ſir, there has been nothing like it.
'Tis eaſier to threaten a blow, than to ſtrike it.
No ſhip has been taken, or frigate, or lugger:
Nor e'en a poor Frenchman for jacktars ———
Though this was a promiſe ſo ſolemnly made
When he call'd on the ſailors to give him their aid:
Yet himſelf he has hid under Gardiner's Iſland,
And ſwears the French ſhips muſt be now taken *by* land.

A

A PASQUINADE.

STUCK UP AT NEW YORK ON THE 25TH OF AUGUST, 1780.

[By STANSBURY; preſerved in 11 Political Magazine, 291.
" The rebels were then carrying off forage, and burning houſes in
ſight of General Clinton."]

HAS the Marquis la Fayette
　　Taken off all our hay yet ?
Says Clinton to the wiſe heads around him :
　　Yes, faith, great Sir Harry,
　　Each ſtack he did carry,
And likewiſe the cattle—confound him !

　　Beſides he now goes
　　Juſt *under your* noſe,
To burn all the houſes to cinder.
　　If that be his project,
　　It is not an object
Worth a great man's attempting to hinder.

　　For forage and houſe
　　I care not a louſe ;
For revenge let the loyaliſts bellow.
　　I ſwear I'll not *do* more
　　To keep them in humour,
Than play on my violencello.

Since

The Loyal Verſes

Since Charles Town is taken,
'Twill ſure ſave my bacon:
I can live a whole year on that ſame, Sir.
Ride about all the day ;
At night, concert or play ;
So a fig for thoſe men that dare blame, Sir.

If growlers complain
I inactive remain,
Will do nothing, nor let any others ;
'Tis ſure no new thing
To ſerve thus our King ;
Witneſs Burgoyne and two famous Brothers !

A POETICAL EPISTLE

FROM JOSEPH STANSBURY TO HIS WIFE.

[Printed from the original Manuſcript, which is dated 'Satur-
day night, 23rd December, 1780.' From the tenor of theſe lines,
we may infer that Stanſbury had come to Philadelphia, and was
waiting permiſſion from the Preſident and Executive Council of
Pennſylvania to return to New York. The jocular reference to
the cauſe of delay may relate to Francis Hopkinſon, Judge of
Admiralty, and the only Judge at the time, who was alſo known
" as a Wit and a Poet beſide," in the city. Mr. Hopkinſon's
witty *Letter on Whitewaſhing* may alſo be alluded to.]

M<small>Y</small> Dear,
     You'll not wonder I'm almoſt in vapours !
This mercileſs, graceleſs detention of Papers—
When my head and my heart were as light as a Cork,
With the hope of a ſafe and quick paſſage to York—
Is almoſt too much for a Mortal to bear !
But Prudence ſuggeſts we ſhould never deſpair ;
And Reaſon points out that Good Humour and
     Patience
Are better Companions than half our Relations ;
Take off the rough edge of illnature and malice
And make our dark Priſon as gay as a Palace.

Tho' kept in ſuſpenſe, yet, my dear, don't pronounce ill
Of Preſident's views, or intentions of Council.
Such baſeleſs opinions I'm ſure you will alter
When once you reflect that a hugeous Defaulter,
A Judge, and a Wit, and a Poet beſide,
For ſome ſmall Offences this day has been tried.

Small

Small Offences! you cry—yes, my dear—and with
  reafon:
For Bribery's nothing compared with Treafon.
And what was this bribe? Why, a glafs of good Wine,
Which all men in office fhould have when they dine.
Whether paid for when bought, or a month or two after,
Might furnifh the court with a fubject for laughter;
Which Judges and Council, a pack of fly elves,
Moft wifely determin'd to keep to themfelves:
Afraid left the Secret fhould 'fcape thro' the key-hole,
The method of changing a Black to a Creole—
Or, if the comparifon is not too trite,
The Secret of making a Blackamoor white!

A Caufe fo important has made me lofe one day; ⎞
Tomorrow muft follow, becaufe it is Sunday; ⎬
And Heav'n only knows what will happen on Monday. ⎠

Thefe Rhymes would fcarce pafs in a Ring for a Poefy;
Yet, pleafe to accept them, as coming from *Jofey*.

INVITATION.

INVITATION.

[By Joseph Stansbury, then at New York. Printed from the original Manufcript, which is dated January 10th, 1781. Thefe lively lines contain fome covert fatire on the royal leaders, and the encouragement they then beftowed on worthlefs feceders from the American Caufe. A clafs of arrivals not enumerated, however, by the poet, is defcribed in the Manufcripts of one of his friends, alfo a refugee at this period in New York.—" Our little half-demolifhed town here feems crowded to the full, and almoft every day produces frefh inhabitants. Two or three days ago, five or fix waggon loads of women and children were fent in from Albany, in imitation of the prudent policy of Philadelphia. It was impoffible to fee them without pain, driving about the ftreets, in the forlorn attitudes which people fatigued with travelling and riding in waggons naturally fall into, making fruitlefs fearches for their hufbands and their fathers."]

YE Members of Congrefs and Councils of State,
   By Rebellion who hope to become rich and great;
The projeƈt, tho' bulky, is lighter than Cork,
Then quit it in time, and come hither to York.

You'll here fee an Army polite and well-fed;
And crowds of fine folks, who lay three in a bed;
With Ladies too wife to be fhut up in Cloifters,
Or live upon Pulfe, when there's plenty of Oyfters.

If Mufters, Fines, Taxes, improv'd beyond reafon,
Or loyal attachment tranfformed to Treafon,
Have wafted your Means or your Patience, come all
Where you'll pay, *for the prefent*, no Taxes at all.

                                        But

But firſt load a Veſſel with lumber, and ſend her :
'Tis true ſhe may meet with ſome Man of War's
  Tender.
My *Shelah* fell in with the *Savage* and *Triton ;*
They ſold her, and left me the ſubjeçt to write on.[77]

If Loyal, come freely—if Rebel, come too ;
Only come *without* leave, it is all you've to do.
Take the Oath, and declare you was forc'd to this puſh ;
And if *York* will not ſuit you, repair to *Flatbuſh.*[78]

You'll there find a country in which you may thrive ;
And two dollars, from you, will go farther than five
From a poor Refugee : and the reaſon is clear—
' It is good to provide leſt the Rebels come here.'

Here plenty of all things for Caſh may be had ;
If that ſhould be wanting, your caſe will be bad.
Yet Money's ſo plenty, you'll find, to your coſt,
That Gold, like your Paper, its value has loſt.[79]

Should Fortune deny you a Mattraſs or Bed,
Or a Cloſet or Hovel to ſhelter your head ;
Conceal your chagrin, and a Volunteer enter,
And ſwear you came here Life and Fortune to venture !

If this ſhould not ſuit you, you may if you pleaſe
·Join freely with loyal and brave Refugees,
And plunder your Friends and your Foes, great and
  ſmall ;
And if you are caught, why—they'll hang you, that's
  all,

        They'll

They'll hang you, that's all—I repeat it again :
And that, you'll confefs, puts an end to your pain.
'Tis what you are ufed to—but *here*, by the Lord !
Theft, rapine and murder may fmile at the Cord.

But, joking apart, all the difference I find
'Twixt this place and that I left lately behind ;
I lie down in *peace*, and in *fafety* arife,
And *Liberty's* mine, an invaluable prize.

So here I enjoy, with unfpeakable pleafure,
The objeéts for which fo much bloodfhed and treafure
Have idly been wafted by both fides, I fear :
And all who would tafte them, fhould wifely come here.

If all in Rebellion would take this advice,
The rupture fo wide would be clof'd in a trice.
Forgetting paft Quarrels we'd happily fing,
Hearts and voices united, *O God Save the King !*

ODE

ODE

FOR THE ST. GEORGE'S SOCIETY AT NEW YORK.

[By Mr. STANSBURY : written in 1781, and printed from his
Manuſcript.80]

IN early Time, e'er infant Law
　　From Wiſdom's bed
　　Had rear'd her head,
The tyrant kept his ſlaves in awe.
　　Juſtice feebly poiſ'd the ſcale :
　　Wiſdom only could prevail.

In vain the aged Matron weeps
O'er bluſhing Beauty's rifled charms ;
　Her eyes on Heaven in vain ſhe keeps :
The fainting Virgin fills the Robber's arms,
Secure he riots o'er his helpleſs prey,
Mocks all her woes, and bears the prize away !

Now brighter days began to dawn.
Oppreſſion ſaw the light, and fled :
In dark Cocytus plung'd her head
　Beneath the infernal wave.
Fair Freedom gilt the ſpreading Lawn ;
Her ſons confeſt a generous flame :
Each ardent Hero pants for fame,
By gallant deeds to build a deathleſs name,
　Or fill a nobler grave.
Immortal Glory high in air
The heavenly ſtandard ſpread !
　　The laurel Wreath,
　　The marble Buſt,

　　　　　　　　　　　　The

The trophied canvafs, and fweet Clio's page
  Defy, O Time, thy utmoft rage.
      The good and juft
      Her fpirit breathe.
'Tis Glory fires the Hero's prayer,
And crowns th' heroic dead.

  Swift at her call in every clime
  Her fons appear in Virtue's caufe;
  Valour fupplied the force of laws,
  And raif'd their fame fublime.

  'Twas thus great George our Patron fhone.
  No Virgin then was heard complain:
  No injur'd Matron fued in vain:
  To diftant lands his fame was known.

  The friend of Man, the Tyrant's foe,
  His bofom felt a generous glow
      To fuccour the diftreft:
  To lateft times are handed down
  His gallant deeds, his juft renown:
      And make his Memory bleft.

  In honor of his natal day,
  His Sons their annual homage pay
      And emulate their Sire.
  Nor fhall their grateful tribute end,
  Till final peals the Heavens fhall rend
      And wrap this Earth in fire.

A

A SONG

TUNE: *The King's Old Courtier.*

[Written by STANSBURY at New York, and printed from his
Manuſcript.]

ON this day our Countrymen, ages before ye,
  Have ſung of St. George, long remember'd in
    ſtory,
The Patron of England, reſplendent in Glory.
    Then Huzza for St. George and Old England!
    St. George and Old England, huzza!

Some Wits have pretended that George, like old Dagon,
Had little of Courage and Glory to brag on;
Himſelf a tame Prieſt, and a Faction the Dragon.

And *Dick*, of good fellows the pride and the life,
Imagined, to keep up the whimſical ſtrife,
St. George was a Bully—the Dragon his Wife.

Tho' this explanation may now raiſe your laughter,
Could he puniſh a Wife, he can puniſh a Daughter,
And all his bad Children, we'll ſhow you hereafter.

He can puniſh his children connected with France,
Who exulting Rebellion's ſtriped Standard advance:
Repenting they ſoon muſt ſubmit to his Lance.

And

And when to their Duty recover'd again,
And humbled the Pride of France, Holland and Spain,
His Flag ſpread in triumph ſhall govern the Main.

Then Clinton and Rodney and all gallant Souls,
Whoſe zeal for their country her fortune controuls,
On this day we'll honour with full flowing Bowls.

And while of St. George with freſh ardour we ſing,
We'll pledge his great Nameſake, our patriot King,
And loud with his Praiſe may the Univerſe ring.
     So huzza for St. George and Old England!
     St. George and Old England, huzza!

ON

ON THE REVIVAL OF THE CHURCH-AND-KING CLUB.

NEW YORK, FEB. 21ST, 1781.

[From the Manuſcripts of JOSEPH STANSBURY.]

WHEN a vile rebel band from Britannia's ſtrong
    hand
  Would fain pluck the Sceptre and Ball,
For our Church and our King we will fight or we'll ſing;
  And with them we will ſtand or will fall.
      Then come let us play,
      And keep holiday
      To celebrate Church and King.

A Club ſo renown'd, with ſuch choice Spirits crown'd;
  Where honour and humour attend;
Should not flag or decay while the Sun rules the day,
  Nor till Time his long journey ſhall end.

Thus united we'll meet, while our Army and Fleet
  The fame of old England advance;
Till from Eaſt to the Weſt we ſtand victors confeſt
  O'er the Congreſs, the Spaniards and France!

When that æra arrives, with our Sweethearts and Wives
  In Chorus we'll joyfully ſing
A hymn to ſweet Peace; may her bleſſings increaſe,
  And ſurround both the Church and the King!
      Oh, then how we'll play,
      And keep holiday,
      To celebrate Church and King!

SONG

SONG

FOR A VENISON DINNER AT MR. BUNYAN'S:
NEW YORK, 1781.

[By STANSBURY: collated from two Manuſcript copies. This
piece was apparently written on occaſion of an arrival of freſh
proviſions from beyond the Britiſh lines.81]

FRIENDS, puſh round the bottle, and let us be
      drinking
While Waſhington up in his mountains is ſlinking.
Good faith, if he's wiſe he'll not leave them behind him,
For he knows he's ſafe nowheres where Britons can find
      him.
When he and Fayette talk of taking this city,
Their vaunting moves only our mirth and our pity.

But tho' near our lines they're too cautious to tarry,
What courage they ſhew when a hen-rooſt they harry!
Who can wonder that Poultry and Oxen and Swine
Seek ſhelter in York from ſuch Valour divine;
While Waſhington's jaws and the Frenchman's are
      aching
The ſpoil they have loſt to be boiling and baking.

Let Clinton and Arnold bring both to ſubjection,
And ſend us more Geeſe here to ſeek our Protection.
Their fleſh and their feathers ſhall meet a kind greeting:
A fat Rebel Turkey is excellent eating:
A Lamb fat as butter, and white as a Chicken—
Theſe ſorts of tame Rebels are excellent picking.

                                        Today

Today a wild Rebel has fmoaked on the Table :
You've cut him and flic'd him as long as you're able.
He bounded like Congo, and bade you defiance ;
And plac'd on his running his greateft reliance.
But Fate overtook him and brought him before ye,
To fhew how Rebellion will wind up *her* Story.

Then chear up, my lads : if the Profpect grows rougher,
Remember from whence, and for whom 'tis, you fuffer :
From Men whom mild Laws, and too happy Condition,
Have puffed up with Pride and inflam'd with Sedition :
For George, whofe reluctance to punifh Offenders
Has ftrengthened the hands of thefe upftart Pretenders,

THE

THE ROYAL OAK.

[By JOSEPH STANSBURY: printed from his Manuſcript, dated May 2nd, 1781.[82]]

WHEN Britain firſt, at Heaven's ſupreme com-
          mand,
  Emerging roſe from out the azure main;
This was the Charter of the favour'd Land,
  And crouds of Guardian Angels ſung this ſtrain:
    Secure while Ocean roars around your chalky
          ſhores,
    Thy Genius ſhall defy each hoſtile ſtroke;
    The Fates for you ordain the empire of the
          Main,
    And Glory hovers over your Walls of Oak.

The Oak, an emblem of your future fame,
  Abides unmov'd the elemental ſtrife;
And one day ſhall acquire a glorious Name
  By ſhielding in his arms great Charles's life.
    Then filling earth and ſkies your mighty deeds ſhall
          riſe:
    No nation then ſhall dare your rage provoke.
    From the Eaſt unto the Weſt, to Neptune's Sons
          confeſt,
    The world ſhall bow in homage to the Royal Oak.

11   Then

Then ſhall the long expected day appear
  When Britain's King ſhall be as good as great;
Rever'd by Foes, and to his People dear;
  The Friend and Father of a mighty State.
    Yet Faction in his days her hydra-head ſhall raiſe,
    And wrap her ſpotted Carcaſe in a Patriot's cloak:
    But Clinton on the ſhore ſhall baniſh'd Peace
      reſtore,
    And Arbuthnot rule the main in the Royal Oak.

Arbuthnot, train'd for half an age to war;
  To face death and danger where glory points the way;
And, often borne on Victory's beaming car
  Enjoy'd the triumph of the well-fought day—
    May he with vengeance fall on the perfidious Gaul,
    And ſtrew their pale-faced Lilies o'er the main;
    That, as they run away, D'Aſtouche himſelf ſhall
      ſay,
    " Begar, me n'engage pas *Royal Oak* again!

WOODLANDS.

WOODLANDS.

[Printed from Mr. STANSBURY's Manuscript copy. Whence its title the editor cannot say. It is dated December 24th, 1782, at which period Stansbury must have been in New York, and could not therefore have written this piece at the Woodlands on Schuylkill, the seat of a brother tory, Mr. William Hamilton.]

WHEN Terror to Madness had near work'd the
    brain,
How sweet to return to cool Reason again !
To find that our hopes in our Country were just :
That Subjects with George might their Liberties trust.

Now Time from the eyes of the Vulgar has drawn
Burke's fine cobweb reasonings—those curtains of lawn.[83]
The Man of the People the People despise,
As children those Toys which a moment they prize.

When Rodney the lucky with his Seamen brave
Stood forth like true Britons their Country to save ;
The conquest to Neptune so pleasing was found,
Their temples with Laurel and Seaweed he crown'd.

And now brighter prospects are spread to our view ;
Fresh honour presaging this Year that is new ;
Indulge we the hope War its horrors may cease,
And all Men enjoy soon the Blessings of Peace.

When

When Peace fhall return here, and bring in her train
Eafe, Love, Joy, and Plenty, to brighten the Plain :
The Sword and Spear be to *Ares* refign'd,
And the Plough, Loom and Sail then fhall comfort
    mankind.

Foul Faction and difcord no more fhall be known ;
But Love, Pity and Kindnefs fhall fit on a throne
To which all around us fhall joyfully bend,
And Peace crown our fhores till the World's at an end.

———

A CHRISTMAS SONG

FOR 1782.

[By STANSBURY : printed from the original Manufcript. The
verfe alluding to Carlton and Wafhington, under the names of
Guy and Hannibal, feems to have been defigned for obliteration
by the poet.]

NOW that Chriftmas-time is come,
    Sound the Fife and beat the Drum :
      We'll live cheerily,
      We'll fing merily,
Now that Chriftmas-time has come.

Be the future Peace or War,
We're refolv'd to banifh Care :
      We'll lay forrow by,
      And tomorrow try
Whether it be Peace or War.

Why

Why ſhould we our moments loſe
For a choice we cannot chuſe?
  Since we cannot tell
  Guy or Hannibal
Conquer will—no moments loſe!

Life, by Fear and Care deſtroy'd,
Longeſt ſeems when moſt enjoy'd.
  Let us live a day;
  And not give away
Whát by Care is ſoon deſtroy'd.

Hope her brighteſt banner ſpreads:
Victory dazzles o'er our heads:
  Britain riſes high,
  Rebel Prizes fly;
Now, while Hope her banner ſpreads.

Soon ſhall Congreſs, France, and Spain,
Wiſh themſelves in Port again;
  While the Dutchman's fate
  Makes him cry too late;
Curſe on Congreſs, France and Spain!

Fill your Bumpers, charge them high:
Britain's name ſhall fill the ſky!
  Prone her foes be hurl'd:
  Peace ſhe'll give the world:
And her Fame ſhall never die!

LET

LET US BE HAPPY AS LONG AS WE CAN.

𝔄 𝔖𝔬𝔫𝔤.

[Printed from the original Manuſcript of JOSEPH STANSBURY, and evidently adapted to the ſituation of the tory refugees at New York, during the latter part of 1782 and the commencement of 1783, when the proſpect was daily growing ſtronger of Great Britain relinquiſhing the War. In this juncture many of the loyaliſts foreſaw the difficulties attendant on their choice of a future place of abode, when the protection of the king's troops ſhould be withdrawn.]

I'VE heard in old times that a Sage uſ'd to ſay
　The Seaſons were nothing—December or May—
The Heat or the Cold never enter'd his Plan;
That all ſhould be happy whenever they can.

No matter what Power directed the State,
He look'd upon ſuch things as order'd by Fate.
Whether govern'd by many, or rul'd by one Man,
His rule was—be happy whenever you can.

He happen'd to enter this world the ſame day
With the ſupple, complying, fam'd Vicar of Bray.
Thro' both of their lives the ſame principle ran:
My boys, we'll be happy as long as we can.

Time-ſerving

Time-ſerving I hate, yet I ſee no good reaſon   ·
A leaf from their book ſhould be thought out of ſeaſon.
When kick'd like a foot-ball from Sheba to Dan,
Egad, let's be happy as long as we can.

Since no one can tell what tomorrow may bring,
Or which ſide ſhall triumph, the Congreſs or King;
Since Fate muſt o'errule us and carry her plan,
Why, let us be happy as long as we can.

Tonight let's enjoy this good Wine and a Song,
And reliſh the hour which we cannot prolong.
If Evil will come, we'll adhere to our Plan
And baffle Misfortune as long as we can.

GOD

GOD SAVE THE KING.

[Collated from two Manuſcript verſions and written by Mr.
STANSBURY, at New York but a ſhort time before the end of
the war.]

TIME was, in defence of his King and the Right,
    We applauded brave Waſhington foremoſt in
        fight:
On the banks of Ohio he ſhouted luſtily
                God ſave the King!
Diſappointed ambition his feet has miſled;
Corrupted his heart and perverted his head:
Loyal no longer, no more he cries faithfully
                Glory and joy crown the King![84]

With Envy inflam'd 'tis in Britain the ſame;
Where leaders, deſpairing of virtuous fame,
Have puſh'd from their ſeats thoſe whoſe watchword
            was conſtantly
                God ſave the King!
The helm of the State they have clutched in their graſp
When American Treaſon is at its laſt gaſp:
When Firmneſs and Loyalty ſoon ſhould ſing valiantly
                Glory and Joy crown the King!

But Britain, with Glory and Conqueſt in view,
When nothing was wanted, but juſt to purſue—
To yield—while her Heroes chanted triumphantly
                God ſave the King!
With curſes conſign to the Furies his Name,
Whoſe Counſels thus cover'd his Country with ſhame!
Loyaliſts ſtill will chant, tho' heavily,
                Glory and Joy crown the King.

                                    Tho'

Tho' ruin'd fo deeply no Angel can fave:
The Empire difmember'd: our King made a Slave:
Still loving, revering, we fhout forth honeftly
        God fave the King!
Tho fated to Banifhment, Poverty, Death, .
Our Hearts are unalter'd, and with our laft breath
Loyal to George, we'll pray moft fervently
        Glory and Joy crown the King!

THE UNITED STATES.

[Thefe lines, by Mr. STANSBURY, are written on the back of his *God fave the King.* Their date is probably about that of the recognition by England of our independence.]

NOW this War at length is o'er;
   Let us think of it no more.
Every Party Lie or Name,
Cancel as our mutual Shame.
Bid each wound of Faction clofe,
Blufhing we were ever Foes.

Now reftor'd to Peace again,
Active Commerce ploughs the Main;
All the arts of Civil Life
Swift fucceed to Martial Strife;
Britain now allows their claim,
Rifing Empire, Wealth, and Fame.

TO CORDELIA.

[Thefe lines were addreffed to his wife by Mr. STANSBURY from Nova Scotia ; whither at the clofe of the Revolution he had retired with many other tory refugees. They are printed from a manufcript copy collated with a verfion publifhed at Philadelphia, in 1805, on page 140 of The Evening Firefide—a literary peri-odical chiefly fupported among the Quakers.]

BELIEVE me, Love, this vagrant life
   O'er Nova Scotia's wilds to roam,
While far from children, friends, or wife,
   Or place that I can call a home
Delights not me ;—another way
My treafures, pleafures, wifhes lay.

In piercing, wet, and wintry fkies,
   Where man would feem in vain to toil
I fee, where'er I turn my eyes,
   Luxuriant pafture, trees and foil.
Uncharm'd I fee :—another way
My fondeft hopes and wifhes lay.

Oh could I through the future fee
   Enough to form a fettled plan,
To feed my infant train and thee
   And fill the rank and ftyle of man :
I'd cheerful be the livelong day ;
Since all my wifhes point that way.

But

But when I ſee a ſordid ſhed
  Of birchen bark, procured with care,
Deſign'd to ſhield the aged head
  Which Britiſh mercy placed there—
'Tis too, too much: I cannot ſtay,
But turn with ſtreaming eyes away.

Oh! how your heart would bleed to view
  Six pretty prattlers like your own,
Expoſ'd to every wind that blew;
  Condemn'd in ſuch a hut to moan.
Could this be borne, Cordelia, ſay?
Contented in your cottage ſtay.

'Tis true, that in this climate rude,
  The mind reſolv'd may happy be;
And may, with toil and ſolitude,
  Live independent and be free.
So the lone hermit yields to ſlow decay:
Unfriended lives—unheeded glides away.

If ſo far humbled that no pride remains,
  But moot indifference which way flows the
    ſtream;
Reſign'd to penury, its cares and pains;
  And hope has left you like a painted dream;
Then here, Cordelia, bend your penſive way,
And cloſe the evening of Life's wretched day.

NOTES.

NOTES.

NOTE 1, Page 1.

ALTHOUGH the date of this piece is anterior to the commencement of hostilities between England and America, its allusions to the "party contentions" which were already beginning to rage, may justify its insertion here. Of the author, Mr. JOSEPH STANSBURY, the editor is not able to give much information. He was an Englishman who had emigrated to America several years previously. The following verses were perhaps the first fruits of his Muse in his adopted land. They are given from a manuscript version collated with that printed in the Evening Fireside (Philadelphia, 1805), page 124; and purport to have been written by Mr. Stansbury on his arrival in Pennsylvania towards the end of the year 1767.

MY NATIVE LAND.

Borne by Eolus o'er the Atlantic waves,
　　To Indian lands unknown I wayward stray,
Whose verdant bosom silver Schuylkill laves;
　　Stately and silent as the close of day.
Where rears the lofty spire its gilded crest,
　　And thriving Commerce drives the busy Car,
In solemn pomp, by liberal Nature drest;
　　Majestic rolls the mighty Delaware.

Tho'

Tho' ſoothing Friendſhip here her healing balm,
　From unexpected hands, benign beſtows,
And o'er life's troubled ſurface ſpreads a calm
　Which lulls to ſilent reſt my former woes;
Still painful Memory prompts the guſhing tear,
　(Her retroſpective mirror in her hand,)
When lively images of kindred dear
　Inſpire the wiſh to ſee my native land.

Tho' manly health with each returning ſun,
　Sheds choiceſt bleſſings on my favour'd head,
And when this buſy varied day is done
　Still keeps his watchful ſtation round my bed:
Yet ſtill, beneath ſevere Reflection's power,
　The numerous paſt tranſactions preſent ſtand,
And Nature's ſtrongeſt ties, each preſent hour,
　Urge me in vain, to hail my native land.

Tho' Wealth, the lordly power by all ador'd,
　Seems kindly to increaſe my little ſtore;
And hardy Temperance with a frugal board
　Forbids pale dreary Want to haunt my door;
Yet will a gentle race of kindred dear,
　Like airy Shades, conjur'd by magic wand,
Ariſe in view, and force a briny tear,
　A tear of reverence for my native land.

Tho' here Religion, heaven-illumined Fair,
　Breathes free, by papal ſhackles unconfin'd;
Prompts from the inmoſt ſoul the vital prayer,
　Alone well-pleaſing to the Eternal Mind:
Still in my, troubled ſight, forever dear,
　Of relatives appear a much loved band;
Nor can my eyes reſtrain the ſtreaming tear,
　While thus they call me to my native land.

Nor

Nor can the tender folace of a wife
  The lov'd idea from my breaft erafe;
Tho' much the dearest treafure of my life,
  Adorn'd with every fweet, attractive grace.
The friendly forms beloved, forever dear,
  Still ftand confeff'd and beckon with the hand:
Adown my cheek faft flows the briny tear,
  While thus they call me to my native land.

Alike the profpect of an offfpring moves
  Life's purple current gladdening thro' my breaft:
The long-wifh'd produce of our mutual loves;
  The fweeteft femblance of a foul at reft.
Yet ftill impetuous gufh fpontaneous tears,
  Like heaven-directed Nile o'er Memphis' ftrand:
To Wifdom's calming courage, deaf mine ears:
  I pant impatient for my native land.

Say, for what new and kindly purpofe given
  This wondrous impulfe, when abroad we roam:
Did Fancy plant it? No, it is from Heaven
  That joy fprings blooming round the thoughts of home.

'Tis this by Liberty infpir'd, adorns
  The brighteft pages of hiftoric truth,
While Afia's Chief his vanquifh'd thoufands mourns
  Before the ardour of the Spartan youth.

No wonder then diftils the pearly tear;
  It ftreaming flows at Nature's high command:
The ties of kindred are forever dear,
  And dear the memory of my native land.

Mr.

Mr. Stanſbury was probably a native of London. In 1785, his ſiſter, Mrs. Collins, reſided at St. Paul's Churchyard in that city. But, from the time of his arrival in America, he appears to have confidered this country as his home. In Philadelphia he eſtabliſhed himſelf in trade; and by his commercial integrity, his literary taſtes, and his many private virtues, ſoon acquired the eſteem of moſt of the chief characters of the city. At a more advanced period his political opinions brought him into direct oppoſition to a number of his perſonal friends: but deſpite the ready wit with which he aſſailed the whigs and even the perſonal adherence that he gave to the royal ſtandard, he ſtill continued to command their good-will. " He uſed to rail without meaſure at the whigs, whom " he held in great contempt," ſays tradition, " but neverthelefs ſuch was his " amiability of diſpoſition and his ſocial worth that even by, whigs of the " firſt ſtanding in politics and ſociety he was prized and eſteemed."

When the Britiſh occupied Philadelphia in 1777, Stanſbury was of courſe one of thoſe who remained to welcome Howe and his followers, in whom he viewed the reſtorers of civil order and the deſtroyers of rebellion. So far as can be gathered now, he had belonged up to a certain period, to the moderate oppoſition: diſſatiſfied with the miniſterial proceedings in regard to America, but totally averſe to a reſort to arms to procure redreſs. There was a large and influential claſs in Pennſylvania who took this view of affairs; and the Declaration of Independence in 1776, was a ſignal for the withdrawal of many (ſuch as the Allens and others) from the whig ranks, even after they had aſſociated in arms againſt England. They would reſiſt us Engliſhmen, not as Americans. By all who came under ſuch a category, the approach of the king's troops was of courſe gladly hailed. By reference to the local newſpapers of the day, we find that Stanſbury on the 10th October, 1777, removed his china ſtore to Front ſtreet, between Market and Cheſnut ſtreets; and that in the ſame month he was appointed by the royal general one of a commiſſion for ſelecting and governing the city watch. On Monday, May 4th, 1778, he was choſen a director of the Library Company of

Philadelphia;

Philadelphia ; and on the 15th of the ſame month, his name is publiſhed with thoſe of ſeveral others of the leading citizens, as a manager of Howe's Lottery for the relief of the poor of the place. On the evacuation of the city, he probably accompanied the fleet to New York, where he continued to dwell during the remainder of the war. During all this period his pen was active in the cauſe of Great Britain, nor did he always ſpare the follies of her friends, while he condemned what he conſidered the crimes of her enemies. All of his productions that can be identified by the editor, and have any political bearing, are given in the preceding pages : the following lines were omitted however in the body of this volume, becauſe though attributed to Stanſbury, the evidence of their authorſhip is purely conjectural. They were printed in Rivington's Gazette—Rivington's *Lying* Gazette, the Americans ſtyled it—March 2d, 1782. Their occaſion was the ſubjoined Epigram, that appeared in the Freeman's Journal (publiſhed by Francis Bailey at Philadelphia), February 13th, 1782, in regard to the title of Rivington's paper having been ſo blurred in the printing as to be ſcarcely legible. Rivington's firſt name was James.

> Says Satan to Jemmy, I hold you a bet
> That you mean to abandon our Royal Gazette ;
> Or, between you and me, you would manage things better
> Than the Title to print on ſo damned a Letter.
>
> Now, being connected ſo long in the Art,
> It would not be prudent at preſent to part :
> And People perhaps would be frighten'd and fret,
> If the Devil alone carried on the Gazette.
>
> Says Jemmy to Satan, (by way of a wipe)
> Who gives me the Matter ſhould furniſh the Type.
> And why you find fault I can ſcarcely divine,
> For the Types, like the Printer, are certainly thine.

'Tis

'Tis your's to deceive with the ſemblance of Truth,
Thou Friend of my Age and thou Guide of my Youth!
But to proſper, pray ſend me ſome further ſupplies,
A Sett of new Types and a Sett of new Lies.

This effuſion was ſubſcribed M.   The anſwer in Rivington bears the letter N: and is ſo inferior to Stanſbury's uſual ſtandard that it can hardly be of his compoſition.

THE RETORT-COURTEOUS.

Says the Poet to Bailey, pray what is the Reaſon,
Since you ſo delight in printing our Treaſon,
That your paper is oft times ſo *ſoft* and ſo *blue*,
That we cannot tell *Tool* from *Fool*, or *I* from *U?*

Says Bailey, the reaſon is plain, Maſter Poet;
Had you one grain of Senſe you ſurely would know it.
Its ſoftneſs reſembles the ſculls of my Writers,
Who're a Sett of nerveleſs inſipid Inditers.

And tho' the Colour's unlike both Chriſtian and Jew Skin,
Yet it greatly reſembles a true Rebel *Blue-Skin:*
Beſides the texture well ſuits ſuch labours as thine,
Which even Minerva can't ſave from Clo'cine.

Perhaps the following extract, from a manuſcript letter from a loyaliſt in New York to a friend in Philadelphia, may explain how the authorſhip of theſe lines was given to Stanſbury. It is poſſible that Bremner was, for caution's ſake, uſed for Bailey; and though the year in which the letter was written does not appear, yet it was certainly not remote from 1782. In reference to ſome encloſures he had received from Philadelphia, the writer, under date of Feb. 26th, ſays: "The German

paper

" paper pleaſ'd ſeveral Heſſian officers and the lines on Bremner ſeveral
" perſons of taſte.   Stanſbury was charm'd with them, and Rivington is to
" uſher them into the world."

While in New York, Stanſbury preſerved the friendſhip of his old
friends among the loyaliſts; and would even ſeem, in December, 1780,
to have viſited Philadelphia.   At the cloſe of the war, he went to Nova
Scotia with a view to ſettling there on the lands aſſigned by England to
the refugees; but the country ſeems to have found as little favour in his
eyes as in thoſe of William Cobbett, and he ſoon returned to the United
States.   Under date of November 14th, 1785, a lady at Philadelphia
writes: " Joſeph Stanſbury called on us the other day: his ſpirits and
" vivacity are ſtill the ſame.   He propoſes living in this city in the ſpring:
" at preſent his family are at Mooreſtown in the Jerſeys, where he ſays any
" body may live."   But if the People at Mooreſtown were willing to forgive and forget, thoſe at Philadelphia were not.   On December 22nd,
1785, the manuſcript laſt quoted from ſays: " Joſeph Stanſbury lives at
" Mooreſtown; but intended to have taken a ſtore here and gone into the
" ſame line of buſineſs as before.   But a fortnight ſince, when he was in
" town, a letter directed to him was thrown into a houſe where he was ſup-
" poſed to lodge.   The purport of it was that he muſt immediately leave
" this city, as he would not be permitted *to live* in it; and ſigned *Mulberry*
" *Ward*.   His friend R. Wells adviſes him to give up the idea of coming
" here at preſent, and go to Wilmington as a place of trade.   Some warm
" people met the evening before the letter was ſent and had ſet in judgment
" on Joſeph's works; his *Town-Meeting* and ſome other performances were
" read and did not tend to cool, but rather to warm; and produced the
" hint to depart.   I ſhould not have mentioned this affair but that I know
" ſuch reports often go abroad with additions, and that it would be beſt to
" relate it as it is.   He is a very obnoxious character with ſome people."
From another ſource I learn that he finally ſettled in New York, where
he paſſed the remainder of his life.

Although there were others of his name in America before the war, it is

not

not known whether they were of the fame family with our author. On the 17th January, 1775, we find *D. Stanfbury*, junior, one of the Committee of Obfervation (whig) for Baltimore county, Maryland ; and the name yet exifts in Baltimore.

With a very few exceptions, I am authorized to believe that the pieces prefented in this volume do not give a fair eftimate of Stanfbury's genius. Although he wrote a great number of poems, &c., during the Revolution, but a fmall number are preferved ; and thefe owe their fafety rather to accident, or to the fact of their being already in print, than to his own inclinations. "He wrote much in the heyday of the Revolution that he "afterwards deftroyed : for with him all refentments died at the clofe of "the ftruggle, and he even feemed to forget who had hated and who had "injured him. His friends he never forgot." The beft authority that I can refer to on this point declares that moft of his pieces collected in this volume were but the creatures of the moment, "Scarce a line of which "he would himfelf have remembered a day after the ink was dry." Neverthelefs, fince fortunate circumftances have enabled me to gather together pretty much all that is known to exift of Stanfbury's writings, I cannot but efteem them worthy of prefervation ; often for their own decided merit, and in every cafe as fignificant memorials of the days gone by.

The only paffage, in the Song that has occafioned this note, which may demand an explanation, is the reference in the fourth ftanza to the difpute between England and Spain refpecting the Falkland Iflands. After all, Spain finally retained undivided poffeffion of the worthlefs but difputed territory. John Adams's letter to his wife of 23rd April, 1776, contains fome curious facts about the St. George's Society at Philadelphia at that day.

NOTE 2, Page 3.

The antecedents of many who, towards the crifis of war, became tories, or at leaft were oppofed to taking up arms againft England, are thus inveighed againft in the Monitor, No. VIII, publifhed at New York, November, 1775 :

The

"The very men who have now luckily fallen into ſuch a pleaſant "dream of loyalty and obedience, in the time of the Stamp Act were moſt "of them 'patriots of diſtinguiſhed note;' the moſt vociferous clamorers "for liberty and property; the life and ſoul of mobs; the leaders in all "the valorous expeloits of plebian phrenzy, ſuch as parading the ſtreets with "effigies, pulling down houſes, tarring and feathering and the like. In a "word, they did not ſcruple in thoſe days to run headlong into practices "much more wanton and diſorderly than any that have happened in the "courſe of our preſent ſtruggle, which has been managed with ſingular "decency, regularity and prudence.

"They then thought it no treaſon, no mortal ſin, no Republican or "Preſbyterian contrivance, to form a Continental Congreſs; to petition "and remonſtrate with ſpirit and freedom; to deny the right of taxation "claimed and exerciſed by the Parliament; to enter into agreements for "the reſtriction of commerce; to act in every reſpect with ſuitable vigour "and reſolution. They did not tremble at the ſound of Miniſterial ven-"geance; neither were they afraid to adopt any deciſive meaſure, becauſe "it might tend to irritate, to widen the breach, to throw an obſtacle in the "way of peace and reconciliation, and the reſt of the trite nonſenſe, the "product of theſe exuberant times. The contracted views of party, the "ſordid motives of ambition and avarice, had not then taken ſuch firm hold "on their minds as they have ſince. They felt the force of reaſon, liſtened "to its dictates, and coöperated in the neceſſary means of bringing ſpeedy "relief to their Country."

Since the above has been in the printer's hand, the editor has been favoured with ſome paſſages in reference to Stanſbury, extracted from the Pennſylvania Records and Archives, which are ſubjoined.

On the 25th November, 1776, at a meeting at the Indian Queen, in Philadelphia, "Mr. Smith attended and informed that he thinks Joſeph "Stanſbury ſung *God Save the King* in his houſe, and a number of perſons "preſent bore him Chorus, on the 15th October, 1776," &c. For this offence, the ſingers were, it ſeems, forced to enter into obligations to con-

fine

fine themselves to their own dwellings: and they probably soon underwent a severer punishment. On December 10th, 1776, the Council of Safety ordered that an enquiry should be made into the causes of the commitment of Joseph Stansbury, William Smith, and others, and that the confirmation or annulment of their confinement should depend on their being found free from disaffection to the Whig cause, and on their taking the oath of fidelity and allegiance to America. On January 4th, 1777, this Council ordered £5 11s. 3d. to be paid Stansbury for glass and delph ware obtained for the Montgomery, a public ship. In the Minutes of the Supreme Executive Council these entries occur: "Phila-"delphia, Nov. 27, 1780. Monday. *Ordered*, that Robert Smith, Esq., "Agent for Estates, do make out an inventory of the goods & effects in his "possession, now or late the property of Joseph Stansbury, and make return "to this Board immediately. * * * Dec. 13, 1780. A petition from "Joseph Stansbury, praying to be permitted to retire within the lines of the "enemy was read, and the same was rejected, so far as it respects his going "to New York. * * * Dec. 18, 1780. On consideration, Ordered, "That Joseph Stansbury, with his family, be permitted to go to New York, "he giving his promise upon honour to proceed immediately to that city, "and use his utmost endeavours to have Abijah Wright & Casper Geyer, "now prisoners on Long Island, released and permitted to return home, "and that he will not do anything injurious to the United States; that his "effects be restored to him, & himself liberated as soon as he shall be ready "to set out for New York; that the agent for confiscated estates be directed "to deliver up the keys of his property. * * * January 8, 1781. On "application, a pass was granted to Mrs. Stansbury (wife of Joseph Stans-"bury), for herself, six children, and a servant maid, with her cloathing, "bedding, &c."

Note 3, Page 5.

"May America prove a sure and lasting Asylum for the Liberties of "Mankind!" (Author's note.)

Note

NOTE 4, Page 5.

Of the hiftory of Dr. ODELL, the author of thefe verfes, I have very little to add to what is already given in *The Loyalift Poetry of the Revolution*, page 199. That he was the writer of *The American Times* (under the pfeudonym of Camillo Querno), printed in that work, is a faft of which I have now no doubt, although it is not there fo ftated, and although it has been attributed to the Rev. Dr. Myles Cooper. In the Royal Pennfylvania Gazette of 26th May, 1778, is a long piece in blank verfe entitled *America's Lamentation*, and fubfcribed C. Q. R.; which letters would more appofitely reprefent the name affumed by the writer of the *Times* than that of any other perfon connefted with the tory prefs known to me. But this does not afford fufficient warrant for its introduftion here. It opens thus:

> O Thou who, with furpaffing glory crown'd,
> Look'ft down from Albion's throne; the fole juft Lord
> Of this new world; to thee I'd fondly call;
> And with a filial voice ftill ufe thy name,
> O Sire, to tell thee how I love thofe beams
> That bring to my remembrance from what ftate
> I fell; how glorious once, under thy fhine, &c.

In regard to the proceedings againft Odell in the Provincial Congrefs of New Jerfey (fee *The Loyalift Poetry*, page 201), it may be added here that when charges were firft lodged with that body, he at the fame time (Oft. 13th, 1775) prefented a prayer that his cafe might be heard that day. He was in attendance on the houfe, and was paroled to return on the 17th; when after a hearing, it was refolved in fubftance that although his intercepted letter expreffed his oppofition to the whig proceedings, yet as that congrefs did not wifh to violate the right of private fentiment, and the letter not appearing to have been defigned to influence

public

public meafures, *etc.*, they would pafs no public cenfure on him.   He was afterwards more ftringently dealt with, in July and Auguft, 1776; doubt-lefs in confequence of his conneftions with certain Britifh officers in June, as commemorated by himfelf in the *Birthday Ode* and the piece fucceed-ing it, *ante*, p. 7.   The remainder of his life was chiefly paffed in New York and Nova Scotia.   The manufcript of a loyal lady who mentions vifits from him at the former place on the 28th Oft., 1781, and 15th Feb., 1782, thus refers to his fettlement in the latter.   "January 5th, 1785. "* * * Dr. Odell I fee is at his deftined abode, and really the Doftor's "profpefts are very flattering.   To hold three or four of the moft lucrative "offices in the Government is not always the lot of one perfon; which will "bring in £1000 *p. ann.*, and is a fituation beyond what he could expeft. "I envy none their profpefts in a new country.   £100 in my native land "with my friends is worth £1000 elfewhere."

In addition to the poetical effufions of Dr. Odell already given, the following pieces may intereft the reader, although from their not poffeffing a political bearing they could not well be inferted previoufly.   They are printed from manufcript copies, and now, it is believed, for the firft time. The fubjoined verfes were doubtlefs addreffed to the corps in which he had once ferved.

A WELCOME HOME TO THE TWENTY-THIRD REGIMENT

AFTER THE PEACE OF 1763.

From burning fands or frozen plains,
    Where Viftory cheer'd the way,
Hail, ye returning, fmall remains
    Of many a glorious day!

In eight revolving years, alas,
    What havoc war has made?
A tear fhall fwell one circling glafs
    In memory of the Dead.

With

With Engliſh hearts, to fate reſign'd,
    They earn'd a deathleſs fame :
For England bled, and left behind
    A ſadly-pleaſing name.

On many a widely diſtant land,
    Or in the howling deep,
Tho' now they ſeem by Death's cold hand
    Held in eternal ſleep :

Yet are they far from what they ſeem ;
    Their *clay* alone is cold :
The *ſoul*, a warm, etherial beam,
    No power of Death can hold.

This mortal frame is but a Screen
    Between us and the Skies ;
Death draws the Curtain, and the Scene
    Then opens on our eyes.

'Tis we that *dream*, not they that *ſleep :*
    Their hovering Spirits fly
Around you ſtill, and on you keep
    A friendly watchful eye.

And thus the Chief, who lately led
    Your courage to the field,
May ſtill be fancied at your head ;
    Still warn you not to yield.

Your loſt companions thus may ſtrive
    With you each toil to bear :
May ſtill in Fancy's eye ſurvive
    Your future fame to ſhare !

with

With joyful triumph, then, review
   Your toils and dangers paſt ;
Fill up the circling glaſs anew,
   And—Welcome home at laſt !

Theſe verſes muſt alſo have been written during Odell's reſidence at London : the alluſions to Pope's works need no explanation.

ON POPE'S GARDEN AT TWICKENHAM : 1765.

Behold the conſecrated Bowers
   Where oft, with rapture ſweet,
The Muſe beguil'd the lingering hours,
   And cheer'd her Bard's retreat.

" To wake the Soul, the Genius raiſe,
   " And mend the Heart," he ſings :
Echo repeats the melting lays ;
   And Fame her tribute brings.

Here nothing ſplendid, nothing great
   Your admiration claims :
No proud diſplay of wealth or ſtate
   Your envy here inflames.

No vain ſepulchral pomp is here ;
   But every paſſing eye
Here pays the tribute of a tear,
   And every heart a ſigh.*₊*

No breathing marbles do you meet
   Near this enchanting ſpot ;
But Inſpiration holds a ſeat
   In yon Muſe-haunted grot.

₊ A plain Obeliſk, to the Memory of Mrs. Pope, with this inſcription : *Ah Editha, Matrum optima, Mulierum amantiſſima, Vale !*

Delightful

Delightful Hermitage ! where ſtill
   Some nameleſs charm reſides :
But ah ! no more the murmuring rill
   Acroſs the cavern glides.

The Genius of the grotto fled ;
   And left the mournful ſtream,
No longer by the Muſes fed,
   To vaniſh as a dream.

Yet here entranc'd a ſimple Swain
   With rapture ſeems inſpired.
Here Fancy liſtens to the ſtrain
   That firſt my boſom fired.

Methinks I hear in every tree
   The fluttering Sylphs around ;
And lo ! the raviſh'd lock I ſee,
   A conſtellation crown'd !

Here, ſhelter'd by the ſolemn ſhade,
   The *Cloiſter* ſeems to riſe,
Where *Eloiſa*, hapleſs Maid,
   Still vents her tender ſighs.

Here, ſhrouded in a bloody vail,
   A more ill-fated Fair
Glides by, and ſwells the hollow gale
   With ſhrieks of wild deſpair.

But hark ? an *evangelic* ſong
   Reechoed from the Spheres,
Here floats the ſilver Thames along :
   " A God, a God appears !"

With

With awful and ſublime delight
This hallow'd ground I tread ;
Where Angels hover in my ſight,
And whiſper o'er my head.

The next piece was evidently compoſed during the ſtorm of the revolutionary war.

MOLLY ODELL ON HER BIRTHDAY.

BY HER FATHER.

Amidſt the rage of civil ſtrife,
The orphan's cries, the widow's tears,
This day my riſing dawn of life
Has meaſured five revolving years.

Unconſcious of the howling ſtorm,
No ſigns of ſhipwreck'd peace I ſee ;
For what, with all its buſtling ſwarm,
What is the noiſy world to me ?

My needle and my book employ
The buſy moments of my day ;
And, for the reſt, with harmleſs joy,
I paſs them in a round of play !

And if, ere long, my vacant heart
Is to be fill'd with Care and Pain,
Still I ſhall bravely bear my part
While Truth and Innocence remain.

With

With one more poem, this felection from Odell's mifcellaneous manufcripts muft terminate. The enfuing is chofen as partaking of an auto-
biographical character.

ON OUR THIRTYNINTH WEDDING-DAY;
6TH OF MAY, 1810.

Twice nineteen years, dear Nancy, on this day
. Complete their circle, fince the fmiling May
Beheld us at the altar kneel and join
In holy rites and vows, which made thee mine.
Then, like the reddening Eaft without a cloud,
Bright was my dawn of joy. To Heaven I bowed
In thankful exultation, well affured
That all my heart could covet was fecured.

But ah, how foon this dawn of Joy fo bright
Was followed by a dark and ftormy night!
The howling tempeft, in a fatal hour,
Drove me, an exile from our nuptial bower,
To feek for refuge in the tented field,
Till democratic Tyranny fhould yield.
Thus torn afunder we, from year to year,
Endured the alternate ftrife of Hope and Fear;
Till, from Sufpenfe deliver'd by Defeat,
I hither came and found a fafe retreat.

Here, join'd by thee and thy young playful train,
I was o'erpaid for years of toil and pain.
We had renounced our native *hoftile* fhore;
And met, I truft, *till death to part no more!*
But faft approaching now the verge of life,
With what emotions do I fee a Wife
And Children, fmiling with affection dear,
And think—how fure that parting, and how near!

The

The ſolemn thought I wiſh not to reſtrain:
Tho' painful, 'tis a ſalutary pain.
Then let this verſe in your remembrance live,
That, when from life releaſed, I ſtill may give
A token of my love; may whiſper ſtill
Some fault to ſhun, ſome duty to fulfill;
May prompt your Sympathy, ſome pain to ſhare;
Or warn you of ſome pleaſures to beware;
Remind you that the Arrow's ſilent flight,
Unſeen alike at noon or dead of night,
Should cauſe no perturbation or diſmay,
But teach you to enjoy the paſſing day
With dutiful tranquillity of mind;
Active and vigilant, but ſtill reſign'd.
For our Redeemer liveth, and we know,
How or whenever parted here below,
His faithful ſervants, in the Realm above,
Shall meet again as heirs of his eternal love.

The Inſcription on Franklin's Stove was undoubtedly written by Dr. Odell. Independently of the aſſertion of his family, and the fact of a manuſcript verſion in his handwriting, dated 1776, being now before me, abundant evidence of his authorſhip will be found in contemporaneous authorities. It is ſo ſtated in the Gentleman's Magazine for April, 1777; in Towne's Evening Poſt; Philadelphia, Nov. 29th, 1777; in Bourcher's View of the American Revolution (London, 1797), p. 449; and in Rev. W. Smith's Works (Philadelphia, 1803), App. to Sermon on Franklin. But Judge Yeates, writing from Lancaſter in December, 1777, attributes it to Miſs Deborah Norris; and a general tradition in Philadelphia aſcribes it either to that lady, or her townſwoman Miſs Hannah Griffitts (See 11 Mems. Hiſt. Soc. Penn., pt. 2; p. 91); both of them of repute as authors. Nor were theſe the only ſatiric verſes in which Franklin's lightning-rods figured. The reader will call to mind how

Peter

Peter Pindar rung the changes on the preference beſtowed by George III and Sir Joſeph Banks upon blunt over pointed conductors; the latter having been recommended by Franklin and the laws of nature as excluſively ſuitable for protection againſt electricity. And as for Odell's cenſure of Franklin's political courſe, it may, howſoever erroneous, be extenuated by the eſtimation in which the latter was held by as warm a whig as the former was a loyaliſt. In 1772, Arthur Lee wrote from London, to Samuel Adams, that Franklin (who was then in that city) was the tool and not the dupe of Lord Hillſborough's deſigns againſt the charter of Maſſachuſetts. Several years after, Lee deliberately explains the circumſtances under which he made that ſtatement: "That he could be " deceived as to the deſigns of the adminiſtration, I could hardly believe. " That he was bribed to betray his truſt I had not ſuſpected. It remained, " therefore, as the moſt probable conjecture, that he endeavoured to lull his " conſtituents into ſecurity, that he might prevent any commotions which " would hazard the lucrative poſts he poſſeſſed. From whatever motive " the deception ſprang, the miſchief of it was ſuch as rendered a counter- " action of it neceſſary. For that purpoſe, the following letter was written; " but it was written in anger, and yet the experience I have had ſince " would juſtify the worſt interpretation of his conduct."—*Lee's A. Lee;* 1, 216, 257.

Note 5, Page 6.

In the abſence of any authority of reference concerning Mr. Piercy, I am induced to add ſuch notices of him as occur to my hand. He belonged to the methodiſt branch of the Church of England, and was one of the few of that claſs who oppoſed the cauſe of the crown. John Adams, then a delegate to the Congreſs ſitting at Philadelphia, mentions him in his Diary under date of Sunday, Oct. 23rd, 1774: "Heard Mr. " Piercy, at Mr. Sproat's. He is chaplain to the Counteſs of Hunting- " don, comes recommended to Mr. Cary, of Charleſtown, from her, as " a faithful ſervant of the Lord; no genius, no orator." He afterwards

paſſed

15*

paffed to the fouthward, and in February, 1778, is mentioned by Elkanah Watfon *(Memoirs; p. 53)*, as having been left by Whitfield in charge of the Orphan Houfe at Bethefda, in Georgia. "We found the family of "Mr. Piercy highly refined and intelligent, and enjoyed their kind hofpi- "tality with much intereft. Meeting people of their cultivation and "delicacy in this remote and folitary abode, was the fource to us of equal "furprife and gratification. The religious duties of the evening were per- "formed with great folemnity and impreffivenefs. At the ringing of a "fmall bell, the negroes, with their children, all came to unite with the "family in their devotions." Dr. Piercy was during the war a good deal in Charlefton, preaching to and encouraging the American troops. Con- fequently, on the fall of the city in 1780, he was ordered to relinquifh his clerical duties; and as his name does not figure among thofe of the "two hundred and ten moft refpectable inhabitants" who addreffed Sir Henry Clinton in June, 1780, we may conclude that he took no pains to conciliate the new authorities. In this fame year we find the "Rev. "Wm. Piercy, clerk," included as a rebel in the difqualifying act of the tory legiflature of Georgia.

Paffing to England, he foon managed to break with his ancient pa- tronefs, Selina, countefs dowager of Huntingdon, as appears from one of his letters, dated Woolwich in Kent, April 3rd, 1784, now before me. He afcribes the caufe to "the attempt to raife a new *Sect* or *Party*, "under her Ladyfhip's patronage, called by the fine name of *Seceders*, alias "*Self-created Bifhops*. But as I did not chufe to expofe myfelf to the juft "contempt of all ferious men of all denominations, I ftand now totally "unconnected with her Ladyfhip: as fhe ftands entirely unconnected with "dear Mr. Whitefield's places and all his people. This has fo much dif- "pleafed the Countefs, that, with her great age and all together, fhe now "refufes to fulfill the folemn engagements made with me in the year ——; "which was to allow me an handfome falary as long as I was her minifter "and chaplain abroad, together with full and honourable compenfation for "One Hundred a year, fettled on me for life, that I was under the neceffity "of

" of forfeiting on her account, when I firſt left this Kingdom. In one of
" the laſt letters which paſſed between us, ſhe informed me ſhe was on the
" point of giving up Bethefda to the States. Indeed, ſhe never will do
" anything ſatiſſactorily with it, ſo as to fulfill Mr. W.'s Will; ſo that, in
" every view, the State had better have it at once, than ſuffer the whole
" Eſtate and Charity to lay waſte."

Dr. Piercy ſubſequently returned to Charleſton, and in 1809-10 was
preſſing his claim againſt Lady Huntingdon on the Bethefda property.
" If you cannot obtain thoſe negroes for me, the ſole property of the
" Counteſs," he writes, " I hope, beſides the ſpecific propoſition for £500,
" you will try hard to obtain the ſpecific intereſt upon the note." In 1812
he returned to England, where he ſoon after died. It is told of Dr. Piercy
that being called on by ſeveral of his congregation, during a period of ex-
ceſſive rains, to offer up in his church the accuſtomed prayer for fair
weather, he replied, after conſiderable heſitation and thumbing of the
almanac, that he would certainly do as they wiſhed; but that the whole
experience of his miniſtry taught him that all the prayers in the world would
be inefficacious to procure an alteration in the weather until the moon
changed. For more concerning him ſee *The Life of Lady Huntingdon;*
volume ſecond.

Note 6, Page 7.

This feſtivity is thus alluded to in the Diary of James Craft of Burlington, as publiſhed in the Hiſtorical Magazine, vol. 1; page 301: " 1776,
7 mo. 13. The Engliſh Priſoners, nearly 90 of 'em ſent off guarded by
" 18 men. They came here about the 26th of 4 mo. laſt. They had
" their Band of Muſick in the Iſland on the 4th of 6th mo. And that
" had liked to have made a Rumpus." Probably Major (then Lieutenant
Andre) was one of theſe. They were removed from Burlington, as being
too nearly within reach of Howe, and ſent to the interior of Pennſylvania.
Under date of July 14th, 1776, Marſhall's Remembrancer ſays: " Yeſter-
" day came to town about eighty priſoners taken at St. John's, on their
" way, it's ſaid, to Cumberland County."

Note

NOTE 7, Page 14.

Due allowance for the power of the poet's imagination muſt be made while reading his panegyric on Queen Charlotte and her "blooming heavenly line." Wolcott paints her majeſty as

———— a downright ſlop
Form'd of the coarfeſt rags of Nature's ſhop;

and greatly lamented that "fierce George Hardinge," her Solicitor, deterred him from doing fuller juſtice to her ſordid traits. As for the children of the king and queen, there was certainly nothing very "heavenly" in the minds and morals of ſome of them.

NOTE 8, Page 14.

The manner in which the Declaration of Independence was celebrated at the city where it was enaĉted and in the earlieſt years of the war, is a matter of ſome intereſt.

On the 5th of July, 1776, Congreſs ordered that copies of the Declaration ſhould be tranſmitted to the ſeveral Aſſemblies, Conventions, Council_s of Safety, &c., that it might be properly proclaimed. On the 6th this Reſolve was received by the Philadelphia Council of Safety, which ordered " that the Sheriff of Philadelphia read, or cauſe to be read and proclaimed " at the State Houſe, in the City of Philadelphia, on Monday, the 8th day " July, inſtant, at twelve o'clock at noon of the ſame day, the Declaration " of the Repreſentatives of the United States of America, and that he " cauſe all his Officers, and the Conſtables of the ſaid City, to attend the " reading thereof." The Council likewife reſolved to attend the reading in a body, and to invite the Committee of Inſpeĉtion to be preſent. In the latter Committee it was, on the 6th, reſolved ſo to attend. " At the " ſame time, the King's Arms there are to be taken down by nine Aſſo- " ciators, here appointed, who are to convey it to a pile of caſks ereĉted " upon the commons, for the purpoſe of a bonfire, and the arms placed
" or

" on the top." As the public election for members of the State Convention was to come off on the 8th, at the State House, this measure was
opposed, left the election might thereby be disturbed, but it was carried
in the committee by a majority.

Accordingly, on Monday, the 8th of July, 1776, " in the presence of
" a great concourse of people, the Declaration of Independence was read
" by John Nixon. The company declared their approbation by three
" repeated huzzas. The King's Arms were taken down at the Court
" Room, State House, at the same time. From there some of us went
" to B. Armitage's tavern; stayed till one. I went and dined at Paul
" Fooks's; lay 'down there after dinner till five. Then he and the
" French engineer went with me on the commons, where the same was
" proclaimed at each of the five Battalions. * * * Fine starlight, pleasant
" evening. There were bonfires, ringing bells, with other great demon-
" strations of joy upon the unanimity and agreement of the declaration."

On the night of Friday, July 4th, 1777—the first anniversary of our
national jubilee—we are told by the Philadelphia newspapers of the time,
that " there was a grand exhibition of fireworks (which began and con-
" cluded with thirteen rockets) on the commons, and the city was beau-
" tifully illuminated. Every thing was conducted with the greatest order
" and decorum, and the face of gladness and joy was universal." Not a
word is said in their news columns of any of those episodes that usually
attend a civic illumination not entirely popular: and it was notorious that
a very large part of the inhabitants, especially of the Quakers, were more
or less secretly hostile not only to the principles but the measures of the
party in power. The Friends in particular would not voluntarily give
either passive or active encouragement to the orders of Congress; and had
brought themselves into general notice by their refusal to comply with
the recommendation for a General Fast, and suspension of business on the
17th May, 1776; by their murmurings against the new order of things;
and by their indisposition to remove their effects from the city in December, 1776, when the threatened approach of Howe put all the whigs to
transporting

tranſporting their effects to places of ſafety. "The Friends here," ſays Marſhall, "moved but little of their goods, as they ſeem to be ſatisfied "that if Gen. Howe ſhould take this City, as many here imagined that "he would, their goods and property would be ſafe." To be ſure there were many Friends who took up arms for America; but as theſe were almoſt all expelled from the Society for ſo doing, their conduct ſerved only to make that of their old comrades more objectionable. Accordingly the celebration of the 4th of July, 1777, might reaſonably have been expected to involve ſome local diſturbances. The following letter from George Bryan, a diſtinguiſhed whig, to his wife, will give ſome notion of the proceedings of the occaſion.

PHILADELPHIA, 4th July, 1777.

My partner and friend :

It is now near eight in the evening. This has been a day of feaſting and the anniverſary of independence, which has, as ſuch, been much noticed. I am juſt returned from dining with Congreſs at the City Tavern. * * * We have ordered out conſtables and watchmen, and expect two hundred ſoldiers to patrole, and that all illuminations and bonfires are to be put out at eleven this night. Perhaps ſome diſorders may happen, but we were willing to give the idea of rejoicing its ſwing, The ſpirits of the whigs muſt be kept up.

One thouſand Carolinians paraded under arms in Second ſtreet, and were reviewed by Congreſs and Generals Gates and Arnold. Two companies of artillery and a company of Georgian foot performed a *feu de joie*. The Maryland light horſe attended and were reviewed. The gallies and ſhips came up and paid their compliments. I am, my deareſt madam, your moſt devoted lover and partner and friend.

GEORGE BRYAN.

Mr. Bryan's anticipations were well-founded. Although, as has been ſuggeſted the local newſpapers were perhaps under a too ominous preſſure of whig bayonets to venture on publiſhing anything likely to injure the cauſe, there neverthelesſ appears, in the Philadelphia Evening Poſt of 5th

July,

July, fide by fide with the " order and decorum " paragraph above quoted, an advertifement fubfcribed Daniel Humphreys, denouncing ' a banditti,' " headed by three certain perfons " and a band of mufic, that had broken his windows, &c.   On the 12th, Richard Peters in another advertifement replied to this ftatement; and affuming that himfelf and two others holding public employments under Congrefs were the " three certain perfons " referred to, altogether denied his complicity.   From all this, and from the paffages to follow, it may be inferred that there was a pretty general affault upon the houfes of fuch obnoxious charaéters in the city as refufed to light up their windows on the night of July 4th, 1777.   The newf-papers contain nothing further on the fubjeét; but the records of the Monthly Meeting of Friends at Philadelphia for the Southern Diftriét, 30th, 7th month (July), 1777, contain a report of the Committee " to " advife and affift fuch of our members who might be fubjeéted to fuffering " for the teftimony of truth," which in a meafure fupplies the deficiency. " And likewife on the evening a day lately appointed by the prefent " powers for public rejoicing, divers Friends had their windows broken " by a licentious mob, becaufe they could not join with the multitude in " illuminating their windows.   But no account has been brought in by " any Friend of the lofs or damage they fuftained."   And in the Northern Diftriét there is a fimilar record.   In both, their blankets had been forci-bly taken from them on a public requifition, " declared to be for fitting " out men to go to war."   This was in confequence of the local authori-ties having appointed a committee to colleét in the city and county of Philadelphia 1334 blankets for the army.   · The committee was empowered to direét the proportion to be taken from any family, on payment of an appraifed value : but to fuch of the Quakers as would not receive Con-tinental Paper Money, this payment was no great matter.   " The being " compelled," continue the Quakers, " into a contribution for fuch a " purpofe has been grievous to honeft minds.   And fome have had their " ftock of this neceffary article fo reduced, as to be likely to want the " needful covering in a cooler feafon."   Thefe trials they fay they endure
" with

" with a good degree of patience and meeknefs ;" and then recite the impofition of having foldiers billeted on them ; their dwellings abufed, and their windows broken, &c. ; " becaufe Friends could not illuminate " their houfes, and conform to fuch vain practices, and outward marks of " rejoicing, to commemorate the time of thefe people's withdrawing " themfelves from all fubjection to the Englifh government, and from an " excellent Conftitution, under which we long enjoyed peace and prof- " perity."—*Almon's Remembrancer ;* v, 292. *Gilpin's Exiles ;* 294.

It was probably becaufe of the troubles of this night that, the next year, Congrefs and the Council forbade any illumination at Philadelphia on July 4th, 1778 ; " on account of the exceffive heat of the weather, the " prefent fcarcity of candles, *and other confiderations.*" The billeting of foldiers referred to above was probably that mentioned by Marfhall, under date of January 25th, 1777 : " Great quantities of backwoodfmen " coming to town this day : fo many that with what were here before, " an order was iffued for the billeting of them in the non-affociators' " houfes, which was put into execution in our part of the city." The non-affociators were fuch as would not take up arms for America.

Note 9, Page 15.

Of General Gates and Judge Richard Peters, it can fcarcely be necef- fary to fay anything. The latter was born in 1744, and was during a great part of the revolution a member of the Board of War. He was always diftinguifhed for his pleafantries ; and acquired a more enduring reputation as a jurift during thirty-fix years of fervice on the bench of the Diftrict Court of Pennfylvania, to which poft he was appointed by Wafhington.

Note 10, Page 15.

James Meafe was born at Strabane, County Tyrone, Ireland ; but came to Philadelphia before the commencement of the revolutionary troubles.

troubles. He was a warm whig from the outſtart; one of the originators of the Firſt City Troop, which did ſuch good ſervice at Trenton, and which has never ſince loſt its organization; and in 1777, Clothier-General of the American Armies. In 1780 we find him ſubſcribing £5000 for the relief of the troops. In later years he did not eſcape the ſatiric laſh of Cobbett. See *Porcupine's Works;* XI: 246, 248.

NOTE 11, Page 15.

Richard and Thomas Willing, two prominent citizens of Philadelphia; one of them (Thomas) was a partner in the houſe of Willing and Morris, and of courſe connected with the extenſive undertakings for furniſhing ſupplies to the army in which Robert Morris was ſo largely engaged. The trait alluded to in the verſe to which this note refers is alſo recorded by John Adams in his Diary for Sunday, 11th September, 1774: " Dined at Mr. Willings. * * * A moſt ſplendid feaſt again—turtle and " every thing elſe." There are few things in his Works more amuſing than the ſurpriſe and pleaſure which, at this period of his life, Mr. Adams exhibits at the ſtyle of living he encountered in the colonies ſouth of New England. He rarely riſes from the table without chronicling its equipage with a particularity worthy of old Pepys himſelf; and though he was undoubtedly willing, as he ſaid, to ſubſiſt at Braintree in the utmoſt frugality; to " eat potatoes, and drink water," if the ſtruggle for freedom ſhould bring him to that neceſſity, yet it is not probable that he would not prefer to live as he was living at the time (1774) he made this pro- feſſion—going " to dine with ſome of the nobles of Pennſylvania at four " o'clock, and feaſt upon ten thouſand delicacies, and ſit drinking Madeira, " Claret and Burgundy till ſix or ſeven." At this period there was pro- bably a conſiderable difference between the eaſtern and the middle colonies in their ſtyle of living. —

NOTE

16

Note 12, Page 15.

This paffage relates to the Conftitution of Pennfylvania framed in 1776 by a convention not regularly authorized fo to do; yet under which the State was governed for feveral years. In his animadverfions upon it, the tory fatirift has more reafon than in moft of his philippics. Graydon fays that its principal authors were George Bryan and a fchoolmafter named James Cannon; though Dr. Franklin was fuppofed to have given either his aid or his countenance to their lucubrations; and tradition affirms that it was drawn up in a fingle night. It is unneceffary here to go into a re-capitulation of its details. It muft fuffice to obferve that it differed funda-mentally from the form of government which it oufted; and that it was bitterly oppofed not only by the tories, the Quakers, and the " moderate men," but alfo by Cadwalader, St. Clair, Morris, and numerous others of the moft diftinguifhed among the whigs. Its own limitations fhut out for fome time any change in its provifions, and the whole power of the State was thus vefted in its friends. Thus John Adams, who was no admirer of it, thought it " agreeable to the body of the people;" yet he could not conceal the light in which it deferved to be regarded. " The proceedings " of the late convention," he writes fhortly after it had framed this conftitu-tion and diffolved, " are not well liked by the beft of the whigs. Their " conftitution is reprobated, and the oath with which they have endeavored " to prop it, by obliging every man to fwear that he will not add to, or " diminifh from, or any way alter that conftitution, before he can vote, " is execrated." It certainly had one good effect, in excluding from any political influence every inhabitant of the ftate who was not in favour of the extreme meafures of the party fupporting Independence: but as it alfo excluded many who were in favour of that ftep, and as it was, after all, tyrannical alike in its birth and in its adminiftration, it was a wife proceeding to get rid of it as foon as poffible. To be fure feveral dif-tinguifhed characters, who were averfe to it at the commencement, in time accepted offices under it; but in fuch cafes the purity of their motives muft be weighed againft the foundnefs of their judgment.

NOTE

NOTE 13, Page 16.

'This fong refers to the following epifode in our revolutionary hiftory. As has already been remarked in a previous Note, the conduct of the Quakers of Pennfylvania was, in the earlier years of the war, extremely unfatiffactory to the whigs. Their willingnefs to remain at Philadelphia when the city was threatened by Howe in the winter of 1776-7, and when every one at all active on the American fide was flying with his effects to the country, confirmed the fufpicions already entertained againft them. In March, 1777, John Adams writes from Philadelphia that " more than one half of the inhabitants have removed into the country, as " it was their wifdom to do. The remainder are chiefly Quakers, as dull " as beetles. From thefe neither good is to be expected nor evil to be " apprehended. They are a kind of neutral tribe, or the race of the " infipids. Howe may poffibly attempt this town, and a pack of fordid " fcoundrels, male and female, feem to have prepared their minds and " bodies, houfes and cellars for his reception; but thefe are few, and " more defpicable in character than number." And in the enfuing June, he again reverts to the impracticable indifference of the Quakers: " This town has been a dead weight upon us. It would be a dead weight " upon the enemy. The *mules* here would plague them more than all " their money." Mr. Adams had unfortunately for himfelf engaged in a logical controverfy with fome of the beft informed among Friends on the queftions of the day, and had not come out very triumphantly from the encounter. This may have embittered him againft them. Accordingly in the latter part of the fummer of 1777, when it was probable that Howe would fpeedily rifk a pitched battle for the poffeffion of Philadelphia, the wifdom of fecuring the perfons of all fuch fufpected characters as by wealth or focial pofition might be able to be of affiftance to him, prefented itfelf ferioufly to the whig leaders. Some papers containing the proceedings of a Quaker meeting in New Jerfey had fallen into the hands of General Sullivan, and by him were tranfmitted to Congrefs. Thefe

documents

documents were fufficient to give an opportunity for the fulfilment of the wifhes of many of the whigs; and it was refolved (Auguft 28th) to requeft the Supreme Executive Council of Pennfylvania to forthwith apprehend eleven of the chief Quakers of the city, named in the refolution. The Council did as it was defired, and more. On the 9th of September, it ordered that twenty-three gentlemen named in the decree, fhould be removed to Staunton in Virginia and there fecured. All of thefe were at the time in confinement at Philadelphia, and were generally Quakers; though there were fome Church of England men among them. The allegation againft them was that they had uniformly manifefted a hoftility to the United States; that they had refufed to pledge their allegiance to the State of Pennfylvania and to promife to hold no correfpondence with the enemy, and that they confidered themfelves fubjeets of the King of Great Britain. They were imprifoned, it was further faid, becaufe they would not promife to remain in their own houfes while their cafe was under difcuffion.

Thefe people endeavored to extricate themfelves by *Habeas Corpus;* but the exercife of the writ was fufpended fo far as they were concerned. No expoftulations which they would make, nor any effort to bring their cafe before a court of jurifdietion, availed them. They were dealt with in the fpirit of martial rather than common law; and perhaps the exigencies of the times may have rendered a difcreet exercife of fuch power, advifable. Unfortunately however under the conftitution of 1776 the control of the State was then mainly in the hands of the Prefbyterians, between whom and the Quakers, and to fome extent the Churchmen, there was a long-eftablifhed political feud. This circumftance undoubtedly infpired vindietivenefs on the one part and exafperation on the other. On the 8th of September, Adams thus writes from Congrefs: "You will "fee by the papers enclofed that we have been obliged to humble the "pride of fome Jefuits, who call themfelves Quakers, but who love "money and land better than liberty or religion. The hypocrites are "endeavoring to raife the cry of perfecution, and to give this matter a "religious

" religious turn, but they can't fucceed. The world knows them and
" their communications. Actuated by a land-jobbing fpirit like that of
" William Penn, they have been foliciting grants of immenſe regions of
" land on the Ohio. American independence has difappointed them,
" which makes them hate it. Yet the daftards dare not avow their hatred
" to it, it feems."

In purfuance of the Order above mentioned, the prifoners in queſtion,
with others feized on a like ground, were exiled to Virginia and detained
there for a very confiderable period. Among thofe fo treated was Benjamin Chew, formerly Chief Juſtice, of whom Thomas Lynch had written
to Waſhington on the 13th November, 1775: " I am fure Mr. Chew is
" fo heartily difpofed to oblige you and to ferve the caufe, that nothing
" in his power will be wanting." Perhaps the arreſt of fome of the
number was rather intended to prevent their doing future harm to the
caufe, than in punifhment for any offence yet committed. Among the
names included in the Order of Council is that of Thomas Wharton,
fenior. Thomas Wharton, *junior,* was Prefident of the Council, and, as
fuch, the Chief Executive Officer of the State. It was to him that the
following characteriſtic letter was addreſſed by one of the prifoners, a
gentleman of high ſtanding in the city.

Hopewell, Virginia, March 9, 1778.—I could not have fuppofed that
thou would have refufed anfwering my letter merely on account of its
wanting a little form. That this may not be neglected for the fame reafon,
I now addreſs thee under the title of (being only intended as a matter of
form),

Friend Wharton,

Thee may remember that in the winter 1776 I and my fon Iſaac
were dragged before the Prefident and Council of Safety upon no other
authority than the will and pleafure of a drunken Şergeant and his guard.
On my return home I was very much affected with the thought that a
perfon with whom I was formerly agreeably connected fhould be in a
fituation the moſt degrading of any I could conceive: It being evident
thou

thou waſt under the influence of this military guard. The next day I wrote thee a letter on the occaſion. Whatever then influenced thee not to return an anſwer, I dare ſay thou art now convinced it would have been better to have done it. Hadſt thou thought it worth while to have heard what I could have ſaid on the occaſion, it is probable I might have been uſeful to thee. With regard to our caſe, who have been condemned and baniſhed without trial; thoſe in authority have either not judged at all, leaving it to Congreſs to judge for them, or they have judged moſt unrighteouſly.

Notwithſtanding the account thee gives of thy time being taken up with thy father Fiſhbourne, &c., thou ſigned orders for our removal under eſcort of two of the Troop, dated Sept. 10th, and orders to Col. Morgan of the ſame date to look out for a proper perſon to convey us from Reading to Staunton; alſo a letter to John Hancock reſpecting our application to Council for our detention at Wincheſter, dated 12th of September.

From the above mentioned authentic papers, it is evident thou haſt been our enemy; and well might I ſay in my former letter that with regard to anything friendly, I am at a loſs in what manner to addreſs thee. But to take thee on the ground of inactivity, on which thou pretended to ſtand, but on which in reality thou didſt not—what would it amount to, but that thou would not commit the evil thyſelf, but keep out of the way, and let others do it? A baſe deſertion of the cauſe of the innocent and oppreſſed: but I have already ſhown thy crime is of a deeper dye.

Thou ſigned orders for our removal under eſcort of two of the Troop. Now what evidence hadſt thou againſt us, whereby thou wouldſt juſtify thyſelf in ſigning this decree? Did the general charge of the Congreſs, publiſhed in all the papers, againſt the people called Quakers, convince thee of our guilt? A moſt ſhameleſs performance, and which we could have fully anſwered in a ſhort time, had we been allowed our undoubted right of being heard in our defence. And now I put it to thy conſcience: what could induce thee to conſent to our being baniſhed for life? Thou couldſt not have believed we had been guilty of any crime that could deſerve ſuch puniſhment.

To

To complete this ſcene of iniquity, orders were iſſued from the War Office to our Conductors, not to ſuffer us to diſtribute our remonſtrances. At the ſame time thoſe charges made againſt us, publiſhed by order of Congreſs, were diſperſed about with great aſſiduity. A remarkable inſtance of injuſtice.

A few words more, and I have done. Before thou ſigned this unjuſt decree, did it not occur to thee that thou waſt well acquainted with a great number of us, and that thou knew us to be a quiet, peaceable people, that were by no means likely to be concerned in plots, or in giving intelligence to the enemy? But if any ſuch thoughts took place in thy mind, it is evident they were not long cheriſhed there. Thou ſigned the unjuſt, the cruel decree, without giving us an opportunity of being heard in our defence.

As it is impoſſible this conduct could proceed from the love of juſtice, ſo I think it is not poſſible thou canſt enjoy peace in thy own mind until thou ſincerely repents for the great injury thou haſt done us, and makes us all the reparation in thy power. That thou mayeſt, through the aſſiſtance of Divine Providence, be enabled to witneſs a ſincere repentance and amendment of life, is the deſire of one who, when that event takes place, may with propriety ſubſcribe himſelf thy real friend,

EDWARD PENINGTON.

In good ſooth, any perſon ſeized on this occaſion, whoſe conſcience did not convict him, had great reaſon for indignation; but there was no ground for their fears who eſteemed it a religious perſecution, and in the mind's eye beheld

> Proteſtant Parſons whipp'd and ſcoff'd at,
> Quakers and Methodiſts thump'd and ſton'd.

NOTE

Note 14, Page 16.

The power claimed before the war by the Britifh Parliament, of tranf-
porting to England for trial perfons charged with the commiffion of certain offences in this country; and of in many cafes depriving the fubject of
the benefit of trial by jury; were efpecial American grievances, and are
recapitulated as fuch in the Declaration of Independence.

Note 15, Page 17.

This paffage again refers to the allegation that the revolt in the colonies
was the work of the Prefbyterians and their Congregational brethren in
New England, and defigned for their efpecial benefit.

Note 16, Page 17.

During its colonial exiftence, Pennfylvania had a paper currency to
fupply the neceffities of its people; fpecie not being always fufficiently
abundant. The bills were iffued by virtue of acts of the legiflature, approved by the crown and containing certain provifions for their redemption. They were loaned in various amounts to the inhabitants of the
ftate on mortgage fecurity, and thus readily went into circulation; and
feem really to have been of great fervice to the community. When the
continental paper bills however began to be iffued, very many perfons
refufed to receive them; and of courfe, on Howe's occupation of Philadelphia, their circulation was entirely prohibited. Such of the inhabitants,
however, as adhered to the old order of things, and who had alfo, in all
probability, accumulated a confiderable fum in the Provincial (or as it
was called *Legal*) Paper Money, faw no reafon why this fort of currency
fhould not continue in its former value. Some time elapfed after the
Britifh army was feated in the city before the fleet of men of war and of
tranfports from New York, led by Admiral Lord Howe, could force a
paffage up the Delaware, which was for the period commanded by the

American

American fortifications on the banks: and during this ſtate of ſuſpenſe, as nothing could be ſettled until Sir William Howe was in a condition to keep his communications with the ſea open, the queſtion of the circulation of Legal Paper Money remained undecided. When the fleet finally arrived, it brought quantities of goods to ſupply the exhauſted markets of Philadelphia; and they who had the diſpoſal of them at once declared they would receive nothing but gold and ſilver in payment. If it be true, as the poet urges, that " the merchant-ſtranger " perceived the improbability of Legal Paper Money ever being redeemed, becauſe not only of the lands mortgaged for their redemption being chiefly in the hands of the whigs, but alſo by reaſon of the mortgage-deeds themſelves being withdrawn; there was certainly good ground for their opinion. The citizens urged, on the one hand, that the bills were iſſued under laws ſanctioned by the King; that they had long been the common circulating medium in the province; that their ſuppreſſion would be alike diſaſtrous to individuals, by deſtroying their only wealth, and to trade, by ouſting the only medium adequate to its neceſſities; and that even the army itſelf would ſuffer, if all bills on England had to be paid for here in gold and ſilver. Their opponents, the ſtorekeepers who came by the fleet, were equally perſiſtent, and in the end prevailed. There is great reaſon to believe that Sir William Howe was ſecretly concerned with Coffin, one of the ſtrangers mentioned in the text, and had a large ſhare in his gains: and for this cauſe he may have been willing to diſcountenance a paper-money that would only be valuable so long as he himſelf was victorious.

In the piece to which this note relates, it would ſeem as though Stanſbury had been willing to indulge in a little irony at the expenſe of his fellow loyaliſts, by verſifying the language of a petition to Howe from ſome of the advocates for the reſtoration of the old paper currency, and at the ſame time interpolating the anſwers of its adverſaries.

NOTE

17

Note 17, Page 18.

The year 1759 was diſtinguiſhed in America by the great ſucceſſes gained over the French by the Britiſh. Ticonderoga, Niagara and Quebec were taken, and the way made clear for the downfall of French power in Canada.

Note 18, Page 19.

The accuſtomed night-watch of the city was of courſe inſufficient to preſerve the peace on occaſion of twelve or fifteen thouſand ſtrangers being added to its population; and the firſt days of Howe's occupation were marked by conſtant thefts and burglaries. It was not conſidered deſirable to eſtabliſh a military patrol in place of a civil police; ſo Howe appointed a number of citizens to be Commiſſioners of the Watch, and to increaſe its numbers and efficiency. Of theſe Stanſbury was one. But as the men would not receive their pay in the paper-money, which would buy them nothing in the ſhops; and as the Commiſſioners had no other to give them; there aroſe an opportunity of bringing the matter before the Engliſh General.

Note 19, Page 19.

This muſt refer to an Addreſs of Congratulation to Howe on his arrival at Philadelphia, and to the refuſal of people to ſign it until he had ſecured, ſo far as in him lay, the value of their local currency by placing it, if not on a par, at leaſt in a due proportion to ſpecie as a legal tender.

Note 20, Page 19.

Faithful to their principles, the Quakers of Philadelphia were the only claſs there reſolute not to be moved by the events of war. When Howe actually took poſſeſſion of the city in 1777, their conduct was ſimilar to that which they diſplayed in the preceding year when he threatened to advance

advance upon it through the Jerſeys. Robert Morris has vividly painted the ſcene on the latter occaſion, in a letter to the Commiſſioners at Paris, dated Philadelphia, 21ſt December, 1776: " This city was for ten days " the greateſt ſcene of diſtreſs that you can conceive: everybody but the " Quakers were removing their families and effects, and now it looks " diſmal and melancholy. The Quakers and their families pretty gene- " rally remain," *etc.* On Howe's entrance in 1777, he iſſued a number of proclamations reſpecting the requirements of the army, the police to be maintained, and the like; a complete collection of which is now before me. One of them relates to the occaſion of this Epigram, and as but one hundred copies of it were ſtruck off for poſting, and probably no other examplar exiſts, it is tranſcribed here at large.

" *Philadelphia, October* 31, 1777. Five or Six Hundred Blankets are " wanted for the Troops. The Inhabitants are requeſted to furniſh that " Number to the Barrack-Maſter, who will pay for them, or return them " in a few Days." So ſoon as the fleet got up, it was doubtleſs an eaſy matter to reſtore blanket for blanket; but it is as eaſy to imagine that in ſuch caſes old lamps are generally exchanged for new. It is problematical whether Friends did not feel as ſenſibly the injury of being called on to ſupply blankets to the Engliſh ſoldiery as to the American: but they did not, at all events, complain of it ſo warmly.

Note 21, Page 20.

Many of the circumſtances referred to in this Song, are related in a preceding Note. In order to bolſter up the circulation of the paper money iſſued under the proprietary government, ſeveral hundred citizens of Philadelphia had ſubſcribed an Agreement, dated October 1ſt, 1777, whereby they promiſed to take it at certain fixed rates: an Engliſh guinea to be eſtimated at thirty-five ſhillings, Pennſylvania currency, for inſtance; a Spaniſh dollar at ſeven and ſixpence, and the like. The liſt of ſigners gives ſome notion of the families who remained in town when Howe drew near. Stanſbury was of courſe one of them.

The

The song itself, though set to a jingling nursery air, has its interest as showing how matters were carried on at the time. The Philadelphia market was almost bare of many articles of necessity, and of almost all of luxury, when the British came in. That of New York was in a better condition; and from it and from England cargoes were waiting to be discharged on the wharves at Philadelphia so soon as opportunity offered. Of course the profits were to be heavy; the more so, as being confined to a favoured few. On the 8th August, 1777, a writer from New York says : " For some time past the demand for goods of all sorts, and the " high prices given for them, has made the fortunes of those who brought " out cargoes with them. This lucrative traffic has been confined to a few " favourites, chiefly Scotchmen. It was thought the British Prohibitory " Act would have prevented the arrival, in America, of all British goods; " but so far from it, that Act has thrown the *whole* trade into the hands of " a few who make a monopoly of it. But the departure of the fleet and " army, which has carried off 24,000 people, soldiers, sailors, and at- " tendants, together with a proclamation issued out, prohibiting all inter- " course with the Jerseys, has made trade very dull of late; however, " many of those who came out lately, and have not got their cargoes sold, " are reshipping their goods, to be ready to sail whenever intelligence " arrives of Sir William Howe having made good his landing, where they " intend to dispose of their goods to great advantage." The character of the supplies mentioned in the Song is amusing; and the arrival of the fleet of transports is spoken of as restoring to the docks of Philadelphia their former appearance of commercial prosperity. But there must have been a great scarcity of many of the ordinary staples of traffic before Howe appeared, as may be gathered from the fact of the importation of Irish beef: an article that had been theretofore prized for seastores in this country, but not for consumption on shore, where our own cattle were abundant. " For long voyages," says the testimony before the Embargo Committee in 1777, "Irish beef is preferred in America because it keeps " better : there is not the smallest probability of its being preferred for " the army."—*Almon's Remembrancer*, VIII : 207.

Note

Note 22, Page 22.

If the whigs of America had their troubles during the war, it muſt not be ſuppoſed that the tories ſlept upon a bed of roſes. At Philadelphia even, where there were hundreds ſuſpeſted of loyal proclivities, a tory was held by the whigs in 1774 as "the moſt deſpicable animal in the " creation. Spiders, toads, ſnakes, are their only proper emblem." So long as they continued paſſively loyal, they were ſubjeſted to affronts and indignities, but when hoſtilities became aſtive, they felt the full weight of whig diſpleaſure. It is but fair to add that on their ſide they were not remiſs in ſeeking to injure their opponents. Every record of the time throws more or leſs light on this ſad condition of affairs, the inevitable conſequence of a civil war in any form or degree. Thus Marſhall enters in his Diary, *January* 21ſt, 1777; "Deal of floating ice in the river, ſo " as to prevent the plunder of a number of Tories in the Jerſies (part of " which, it's ſaid to the amount of thirtyſeven wagons, is arrived at Wil- " liam Cooper's ferry, &c.), from being brought over to this city." The tories in New Jerſey were far more aſtive than their Pennſylvania friends. In 1777, we find Alexander Hamilton urging Governor Livingſton to viſit with exemplary puniſhment all ſuch, taken in arms or employed in enliſting men for the Britiſh ſervice: and while Livingſton hanged them for treaſon againſt the ſtate when opportunity offered, Waſhington him-ſelf ſaw the neceſſity of ſtringent meaſures againſt the moſt atrocious offenders, and thus wrote to Congreſs: "In this ſtate, I have ſtrong " aſſurance that the ſpirit of diſaffeſtion has riſen to a great height; and " I ſhall not be diſappointed if a large number of the inhabitants in ſome " of the counties ſhould openly appear in arms, as ſoon as the enemy " begin their operations."

Note

Note 23, Page 23.

Sir William Howe's bittereſt enemies never denied him the poſſeſſion of "thoſe military abilities which were demonſtrated in his manœuvres "on Long Iſland and the Brandywine, and that undaunted courage which "was ſo apparent in the action at Bunker's Hill." But his warmeſt friends muſt have perceived in his conduct of the American campaign, an alloy of ignoble traits that, under Cromwell or Napoleon, would have brought a commanding general to a very diſgraceful end.

In conſidering his career in America it muſt be borne in mind that great reſults were at firſt expected by his brother, Lord Howe, and himſelf, from the pacific powers with which, as Royal Commiſſioners, they were inveſted. It is very probable that Lord Howe, who was a purer character than Sir William, counted a great deal on the influence of Dr. Franklin and ſome other leaders in the American councils in favour of bringing about an accommodation. His interviews with Franklin on this ſubject, while the latter was yet in England, as related by the doctor himſelf, could not have inſpired him with very ſtrong faith in the ſucceſs of ſuch an undertaking : yet we muſt remember that each party may have looked at the event in a different light. It is certain that Lord Howe took every preliminary ſtep that was in his power to gain favour in the eyes of the Americans ; among other evidences of which is the following letter (which I believe has not been publiſhed) from Mr. De Berdt, to James Kinſey, Eſq., of the New Jerſey Legiſlature.

London, May 5, 1776. *Sir :* My Brother in Law Joſeph Read Eſq. having particularly informed me the honor your Aſſembly has done me by chooſing me their Agent in November laſt, and how the obligation was encreaſed by the unanimity of the choice, give me leave Sir with the acknowledgment of the favor to attempt ſome proof of my attachment and regard to your Province and Country.

I would inform you that from public report there was the greateſt
reaſon

reaſon to believe Lord Howe who is going out to America commander in chief of his Majeſties Forces, &ca, &ca, had deſigns the moſt friendly & intentions of accommodating the unhappy differences without violence. I therefore did myſelf the honor to wait upon him and was ſo confirmed in my belief of what I had heard and ſo fully ſatiffied from his Lordſhip's converſation that he accepted his commiffion ſolely with a view to effeɛt Peace, that I cannot help communicating to you a propoſal which I am confident is the wiſh & deſire of his Lordſhip & I think is your duty and intereſt. I do not write this merely as matter of opinion or recommend it as a prudent ſtep only ; but propoſe it from a full conviɛtion of my judgement that it is reaſonable—that it is right—and further I have affurances that it will be accepted and that no unreaſonable conceffions will be requeſted.

And tho' it is preſumable that his Lordſhip's inſtruɛtions are confined within the aɛt of Parliament appointing Commiffioners yet it is generally believed he has ſuch diſpenſing powers that with a diſpoſition to treat he is authorized to compromiſe & adjuſt.

What I mean is that immediately on Lord Howe's arrival a Parly or Conference be propoſed between him and certain Deputies from among you to converſe on the ſtate of public affairs as Gentlemen & Friends.

The general report in England of his peacefull intentions confirmed from private conferences with ſome of your friends who have wrote to you on the ſubjeɛt begging that the matter may be taken into your moſt ſerious conſideration and the particular reſpeɛt which the people of America bear his Lordſhip and Family, added to his amiable charaɛter as an Officer and a Gentleman ſurely a parly may be brought about for ſome ſuch reaſons in which the dignity of his country will not be affeɛted nor the honour of America called in queſtion.

My real regard for America, my wiſh for peace and reconciliation, my faith in Lord Howe's perſonal affurances and my deſire of giving early proof to your honorable Houſe of Affembly that their appointment is fallen upon a Man who will ever make it the ſtudy of his Life to promote

the

the welfare and happinefs of his conftituents, thefe motives & thefe alone influence my Heart & actuate my Conduct.

However infuccefsfull this humble attempt of mine may prove, I beg it may be remembered as a proof of my good wifhes and intentions. I beg you will communicate this to the Houfe, as early as poffible and to accept my affurances of efteem & regard. I am your obliged and obedient hble fervt. DENNIS DE BERDT.

Favored by Lord Howe.

With fuch credentials Lord Howe departed on his miffion, in expectation, no doubt, of procuring an accommodation. In a contemporaneous manufcript notebook of George Chalmers, I find this memorandum: " C. Stewart fays—that Lord H— having been affured by Dr. Franklin, " what would fatiffy the Colonies, made it a point that he fhould be " empowered to grant thefe. He was empowered. He took privateers " on his voyage, but difmiffed them, defiring them to fay; Lord H—was " to make peace. *He told Arbuthnot, at Halifax, that peace would be* " *made within ten days after his arrival.*" Had he arrived in feafon, it is within the limits of poffibility that he might have effected fomething, if we may draw any inferences from the anxiety difplayed by the advocates for Independence in Congrefs to propagate the belief that there were no fuch Commiffioners coming at all; and the attention that was given to the report by others who were not fo warm in that caufe. "We are waiting, " it is faid," fays Adams in April, 1776, " for commiffioners; a meffiah " that will never come. This ftory of commiffioners is as arrant an illu " fion as ever was hatched in the brain of an enthufiaft, a politician, or a " maniac. I have laughed at it, fcolded at it, grieved at it, and I don't " know but I may, in an unguarded moment, have rip'd at it. But it is " in vain to reafon againft fuch delufions. I was very forry to fee, in a " letter from the General [Wafhington] that he had been bubbled with " it; and ftill more, to fee, in a letter from my fagacious friend, W. " [James Warren] at Plymouth, that he was taken in too." But Com miffioners were coming, and it would be rendering flight juftice to New England

England aftutenefs not to believe her delegates knew it. It is not at all improbable, in the opinion of fome, that before the arrival of Sir William Howe at Sandy Hook on the 25th of June, and of Lord Howe at Staten Ifland on the 12th July, the profpect of encountering them as fellow-fubjects and negotiators, inftead of as foreigners and enemies, had been fully confidered; and that the neceflity of committing the colonies through their reprefentatives, to an extent that would put an accommodation out of the queftion, had a great deal to do with the enactment on the 2nd July, of the refolution declaring " that thefe United Colonies are, and of " right ought to be, free and independent States." And accordingly, though the Howes waited for overtures from the whigs ere they commenced hoftilities, and even directly invited juft fuch a conference with members of congrefs as had been recommended by De Berdt (who probably was their mouthpiece in his letter), yet congrefs was now able to point to its record, and refufe to negotiate fave on the footing of independency.

In the warfare that prefently enfued, Sir William Howe frequently difplayed good generalfhip: in fact it appears as though, when he himfelf felt that he *muft* fight, his abilities were fuperior to thofe of any or all of his opponents. But he omitted to pufh his victories, and feemed determined to leave the Americans at leaft the nucleus of an army. After defeating the Americans on Long Ifland, a vigorous night-attack on their works would probably have demolifhed our army; inftead of which, the next day faw them efcaped to the main land. After the reduction of Fort Wafhington, when Greene retreated with the garrifon of Fort Lee left it fhould fhare the fame fate, Thomas Payne, who was with the troops, was of opinion that Howe committed another overfight, in not detaching a force from Staten Ifland through Amboy, whereby Greene's retreat into Pennfylvania might have been cut off, and the American magazines at Brunfwick captured. "But," pioufly adds Payne, "if we believe the " power of hell to be limited, we muft likewife believe that their agents " are under fome providential controul." The criticifms of a civilian on
military

military affairs may not be worth much. Fortunately I have before me a feries of manufcript memorandums by Sir Henry Clinton, on the events and conduct of the war, that may better teft the value of Howe's fervices. Of the meafure that led to the American victories of Trenton and Princeton, Sir Henry obferves: "There were who thought (and were not filent) "that a chain acrofs Jerfey might be dangerous. General Howe wrote "to General Clinton thus a few days before the miffortune: 'I have been "prevailed upon to run a chain acrofs Jerfey: the links are rather too far "afunder.' * * * I am clear," Clinton continues, "it would have been "better if Sir William Howe had not taken a chain acrofs Jerfey."

Of the maraudings in 1776-7 of the Englifh in the Jerfeys, Clinton fays: "Unlefs we could refrain from plundering, we had no bufinefs to take "up winter quarters in a diftrict we wifhed to preferve loyal. The "Heffians introduced it."

Of Howe's movement from New York againft Philadelphia, he obferves: "I owe it to truth to fay there was not, I believe, a man in the "army except Lord Cornwallis and General Grant who did not reprobate "the move to the fouthward, and fee the neceffity of a coöperation with "General Burgoyne."

Of Howe's fuffering Wafhington to retreat, comparatively unpurfued at the moment, from the field of Brandywine: "'Tis pity Sir William "Howe could not have begun his march at nightfall, inftead of eight "o'clock in the morning."

Of Howe's crowning the campaign with the occupation of Philadelphia: "General Clinton told Lord George Germain, April 27th, and Sir "William Howe repeatedly, after his return to America, his humble "opinion that Philadelphia had better clofe than open the campaign, as "it required an army to defend it."

Of the battle of Germantown and the check to the Americans occafioned by Mufgrave's throwing himfelf with a few companies into Chew's Houfe, Sir Henry makes a remark that, while it fhews on what chances the fate of a battle may turn, does not at all fupport Howe's affeveration

that

that his army was not ſurpriſed: "Had Waſhington left a corps to ob-
" ſerve this houſe, and proceeded, there is no ſaying what might have
" been the conſequence."

But enough has been quoted to exhibit Sir William's deficiencies:
what their cauſe was is another queſtion. Tradition aſſigns a baſe motive
to him, in the aſſertion of a deſire to increaſe his fortune in procraſti-
nating the war, through underhand arranegments with thoſe to whom
he aſſigned the privileges of trade, and others. He is ſaid to have been
the ſecret partner of Coffin, a great trader under the royal flag. Harſh
as this ſuſpicion may ſound, it is confirmed by Horace Walpole's language
to Sir Horace Mann, in 1778: "General Howe is returned, richer in
" money than in laurels;" and by that of Adams, a year earlier:
" Theſe two Howes were very poor, and they have ſpent the little for-
" tunes they had in bribery at elections; and having obtained ſeats in
" Parliament, and having ſome reputation as brave men, they had nothing
" to do but to carry their votes and their valor to market, and, it is very
" true, they have ſold them at a high price." During the period of his
command in America, there was ſuch a corrupt miſmanagent of the fiſcal
concerns of his army, as ſtaggered even a Scottiſh placehunter. " The
" peculation in every profitable branch of the ſervice," wrote Wedder-
burn in 1777-8, " is repreſented to be enormous, and as uſual, it is attended
" with a ſhocking neglect of every comfort to the troops. The hoſpitals
" are peſthouſes, and the proviſions ſerved out are poiſon: thoſe that are
" to be bought, are ſold at the higheſt prices of a monopoly." It is eaſy
to ſee how, in this ſtate of affairs, a venal commander might make his
own bargains with thoſe with whom he would combine to defraud his
followers and his country. There is no poſitive evidence, however, that
Howe was guilty in this regard: the only proof we have is ſuch as has
been recited and ſuch looſe aſſertions as that contained in the goſſip of the
times; a ſpecimen of which may be found in the Verſes circulated in
Edinburg in May, 1778, on occaſion of equipping a new Scots regiment, and commencing, *How art thou fallen, poor John Bull!*—in which
reference is made to the Americans

Who

Who force thee from thy native right,
Becaufe thy Heroes will not fight:
(Perfidious men! who millions gain
By each protracted, flow campaign!)

Sir Nathaniel Wraxall fpeaks very plainly of the eftimate he put upon Sir William and his brother; they were "either lukewarm, or remifs, or " negligent, or incapable. Lord North's felection of thefe two com- " manders excited, at the üme, juft condemnation. However brave, " able, or meritorious they might individually be efteemed as profeffional " men, their ardour in the caufe itfelf was doubted, and ftill more quef- " tionable was their attachment to the adminiftration. Never, perhaps, " in the hiftory of modern war, has an army or a fleet been more pro- " fufely fupplied with every requifite for brilliant and efficient fervice, " than were the troops and fhips fent out by Lord North's cabinet, in " 1776, acrofs the Atlantic. But the efforts abroad did not correfpond " with the exertions made at home. The energy and activity of a " Wellington never animated that torpid mafs. Neither vigilance, enter- " prife, nor coöperation characterized the campaign of 1776 and 1777. " Diffipation, play, and relaxation of difcipline found their way into the " Britifh camp."

The fecret of the appointment may have been that North, knowing the profeffional abilities of the men; the efteem in which their relation- fhip to the Howe who was flain in America during the Seven Years' War entitled them to be held in that country; their political connexions with the Whigs in England; and perhaps, their kindred (on the wrong fide of the blanket, it is true—and indeed the fame was whifpered of the premier himfelf—) to the fovereign; was influenced by one or all of thefe confiderations to beftow on them the pofts in queftion. To carry this through, arrangements had to be made in regard to Sir Guy Carleton, the commander in Canada, who was Howe's fenior officer—an older foldier, and perhaps a better; at all events a more zealous and active one. Indeed, fuch was Howe's fluggifhnefs and love of pleafure in almoft every

form

form (ſee *Coll. Hiſt. Soc. Penn.*, 1, 120), that it is no great praiſe to ſay thus much of Carleton. Sir Walter Scott quotes from an old ſong in one of his letters

> General Howe is a gallant commander,
> There are others as gallant as he ;

and in Simcoe, a mere grenadier captain of the 40th, under Sir William's command, the ſtuff might have been found for a leader who, in Sir William's place, would have given a different turn to events. By the end of the winter of 1777-8, the miniſtry gave their general to underſtand that they were very ill content with what he had done, or rather with what he had left undone ; and his pride or his prudence at once took umbrage. He already looked on Clinton as a rival; and had thus addreſſed Lord George Germain on this head : " I am led to hope that I may be re-" lieved from this very painful ſervice, wherein I have not the good " fortune to enjoy the neceſſary ſupport and confidence of my ſuperiors, " but which, I conclude, will be extended to Sir Henry Clinton, my pre-" ſumptive ſucceſſor. By the return of the packet I humbly requeſt I " may have his Majeſty's permiſſion to reſign." When the permiſſion came, however, he diſcovered, if we are to believe that the American general Charles Lee rightly interpreted his ſentiments, that he had all along been made uſe of as an inſtrument of miniſterial wickedneſs and folly. Nothing can be more characteriſtic than the portrait Lee draws of Sir William : " He is naturally good humored, complaiſant, but illite-" rate and indolent to the laſt degree, unleſs as an executive ſoldier, in " which capacity he is all fire and activity, brave and cool as Julius Cæſar. " His underſtanding is, as I obſerved before, rather good than otherwiſe, " but was totally confounded and ſtupified by the immenſity of the taſk " impoſed upon him. He ſhut his eyes, fought his battles, drank his " bottle, had his little ——, adviſed with his counſellors, received his " orders from North and Germaine (one more abſurd than the other), " took Galloway's opinion, ſhut his eyes, fought again, and is now, I
" ſuppoſe,

" ſuppoſe, to be called to account for acting according to inſtructions."
Lee thought that the conflict between Waſhington and Howe had reſolved
itſelf into a trial of the efficacy of their reſpective blunders. " It ſeemed
" to be a trial of ſkill, which party ſhould outdo the other, and it is hard
" to ſay which played the deepeſt ſtrokes; but it was a capital one of
" ours, which certainly gave the happy turn which affairs have taken.
" Upon my ſoul, it was time for Fortune to interpoſe, or we were inevit-
" ably loſt." So far as his treatment of Americans was concerned,
Howe's blunders were indeed capital. He incenſed the whigs by his
ſeverities: he repelled the loyaliſts, by putting as little confidence in them
as might be, and diſcouraging their organization and action in arms; and
he waſted his time in futile efforts to open, through the medium of Sullivan, Lee, Willing, and other whigs, negotiations with Congreſs. He
returned to England unpopular alike with the miniſtry and the nation,
although followed by the applauſe of thoſe whom he had commanded.
Even at Nottingham, his own town, he was not acceptable to the inhabitants. Unlike his brother, who lived to do his country brilliant ſervice
and to add a freſher luſtre to the maritime glory of England, Sir William
was never again, ſo far as is generally known, inveſted with command.
He appears to have ſucceeded to this brother's Iriſh Viſcounty (the Engliſh peerage failing, for lack of a ſon to its poſſeſſor) and died in 1814.

Note 24, Page 24.

Though Diſcord, your generous zeal to oppoſe,
   Shall nouriſh ſedition and hate,
Till your Friends feel the horrors of War with your Foes,
   Your ſucceſs is enſur'd you by Fate.—*Author's Variation.*

Note 25, Page 25.

Hermes' Wand the fierce Snakes could no longer unite;
   Its Virtues they wholly defied:
The branch of the Olive did only affright,
   To ſee it at random applied.—*Author's Variation.*

Perhaps

Perhaps there may be an alluſion here to the broken Snake, with the motto *Unite or Die*, ſo much in vogue at the time as a patriotic device.

Note 26, Page 29.

The efforts of the Philadelphians to obtain the commercial reſtoration of their colonial paper currency have been dwelt upon in a previous note. This poem commemorates the failure of their endeavours.

Note 27, Page 29.

While the ſtyle of Dr. Smith's Oration may have recommended it to the loyal bard, it probably loſt nothing, in his eſtimation, by the circum-ſtance of its author loſing grace in the eyes of Congreſs. "The oration "was an inſolent performance," ſays Mr. Adams. "A motion was "made to thank the Orator, and aſk a copy, but oppoſed with great ſpirit "and vivacity from every part of the room, and at laſt withdrawn, leſt "it ſhould be rejeſted, as it certainly would have been, with indignation. "The Orator then printed it himſelf, after leaving out or altering ſome "offenſive paſſages. This is one of the moſt irregular and extravagant "characters of the age. I never heard one ſingle perſon ſpeak well of "anything about him but his abilities, which are generally allowed to be "good. The appointment of him to make the oration was a great over-"ſight and miſtake." The objeſtion urged in Congreſs to the motion was that the Orator had declared them to be ſtill anxious for a dependency upon Great Britain. The motion was ſuſtained, though fruitleſſly, by William Livingſton, Duane, Thomas Willing, James Wilſon, &c.

Note 28, Page 30.

—Nor loſt or dead or founder'd Horſe :
I would to Heaven it were no worſe.
But fain I muſt your Patience aſk
While I perform the mournful taſk ;
—So mournful, I could weep, *my honey*—
Alas ! the Death of Paper Money.—*Author's Variation.*

Whether

Whether Howe or Mongomery be aimed at in the firſt part of the paragraph referred to by this note, the reader may decide. Perhaps the poet, in no very amiable mood at the time, when Howe's conduct had reduced to worthleſſneſs the moneybags of many of the citizens, may have purpoſely dealt in an ambiguous expreſſion. As to the *Want of Bread* which threatened him and his friends, left thus in the lurch without available funds, the prices that proviſions bore in Philadelphia at that period would ſeem to warrant his alarm. Before the Americans withdrew, the better claſſes had been forced in great meaſure to relinquiſh the uſe ſo Weſt India goods. " Milk has become the breakfaſt of many of the " wealthieſt and genteeleſt families here." Loaf ſugar ſold then at four dollars a pound ; brown ſugar of the pooreſt quality at a dollar ; and New England rum at forty ſhillings a gallon. After the royal army entered the city, and before the arrival of the fleet, beef was at three and nine pence (half a dollar) and butter at ſeven and ſix pence (one dollar) the pound ; and this in ſpecie. And before the winter was over, even theſe difficult times were made more arduous to be endured. In February, 1778, flour commanded three guineas the hundred weight, and all other proviſions were at a proportional rate. Congreſs had made it a capital felony for any inhabitant of Pennſylvania or New Jerſey to ſupply proviſions to Philadelphia, and the American patrolling parties made it an eſpecial point to cut off all ſuch perſons as, tempted by the prices their commodities brought in that market, would ſeek to evade or defy the decree. As the troops were well furniſhed with garriſon rations, this prohibition fell moſt ſeverely on the citizens of the town ; and its rigour forced a parliamentary admiſſion of its injuſtice from Marſhal Conway, one of the ſteadieſt opponents of the Engliſh miniſtry. He ſtated correctly the military principle " that when the hope of ſubduing an enemy " by ſtarving made the penalty of ſupplying them with proviſions *death*, " then thoſe who were the treſpaſſers did it at their peril, and the general " who publiſhed the order was juſtified : but in no other caſe." In theſe ſtraits, the leading Quaker gentry of Philadelphia were, it is ſaid, compelled

pelled to make applications to Dr. Fothergill and others of their perſuaſion at London, for relief, to be repaid at the end of the troubles.

Note 29, Page 30.

With grief the Muſe proceeds and tells.—*Author's Variation.*

Note 30, Page 35.

On the 29th of January, 1778, Sir James Wallace of the *Experiment* (a fourth-rater of fifty guns), brought as a prize into New York the Lady Margaret, a Dutch veſſel of 600 tons, commanded by Captain De Ruyter and bound from Cadiz to Carolina on account of Congreſs. Her cargo chiefly conſiſted in 5000 pounds of Jeſuit's Bark ; wine ; ſalt ; brandy ; cordage ; linens ; tea ; medicines ; and mercer's ware : articles of the firſt neceſſity to our army. The prize was a rich one ; and there was an additional ſatiſſaction to the royaliſts in its detection while engaged in the trade with the Americans that it was well known France and Holland were covertly carrying on.

As for Wallace himſelf, he ſeems to have been a brutal ſort of a ſea-dog ; ſomething after the now happily obſolete ſtyle of Sir Hawſer Trunnion. " His character upon the coaſt was that of being brutal and inſo-" lent beyond his peers," ſays one of his acquaintance : and his behaviour on ſhore was that of a man who would ſwear at a lady and bully a clergyman or a Quaker. On one occaſion, at a ſupper table in Philadelphia, he purſued a Quaker with a deal of vulgar raillery and ſarcaſm, till the latter was tempted to reſort, if not to the weapon of the carnal Adam, at leaſt to that of the repreſentatives of our mother Eve. " Captain," ſaid the " friend, thou haſt made very free with me, and aſked me a great many " queſtions, which I have endeavoured to anſwer to thy ſatiſſaction : wilt " thou now permit me to aſk thee one in my turn ?" " Oh, by all means," anſwered Sir James ; " any thing that you pleaſe, friend—what is it ? " Why, then, I wiſh to be informed what makes thee drink ſo often ?

" Art

" Art thou really dry, every time thou carrieſt the liquor to thy mouth ?"
" What," ſcreamed Wallace in a guſt of rage—"what! do you think I
" am a hog, only to drink when I am dry!" The Quaker retreated
under a volley of oaths, ſatiſfied no doubt with the homethruſt he had in-
flicted.   Wallace was however a good ſailor; and though he and the
Experiment were taken by D'Eſtaing's fleet in September, 1779, he was
ſoon at ſea again.   Indeed the Experiment itſelf is reported as being at
Gibraltar in June, 1780, and in July Wallace himſelf, in command of
the Nonſuch, juſt after completing the deſtruction of the *Legere*, a French
frigate, was ſo lucky as to fall in with and capture *La Belle Poule*, renowned in naval ſong for her encounter with the " ſaucy Arethuſa."   In
1783 he made a ſenſation in London by proſecuting to conviction Mr.
Bourne, of the Marines, for an aſſault, to the unqualified diſguſt of the
corps: which paſſed a reſolve that no gentleman bearing his majeſty's
commiſſion ought to go out with a man who, having been publicly caned,
&c., thought fit to ſeek for his redreſs in a Court of Juſtice.

Note 31, Page 35.

You Tories compare theſe poor devils to Mites, who always deſtroy
the ſubſtance that gives them life and ſupport.—*Author's Note.*

Note 32, Page 35.

The Experiment man of war commanded by Sir James.—*Author's
Note.*

Note 33, Page 35.

Brandy won't ſave them—"as the ſaying is." *₊* The Ship's Cargo
conſiſted of the above mentioned articles.—*Author's Note.*

Note

Note 34, Page 36.

Such aſſociations as the Church-and-King club were not of unuſual occurrence with the loyaliſts. They were generally deſigned to bring together at the dinner table a party of men whoſe political ſentiments were in uniſon. In this inſtance, the members were probably Philadelphians, who had followed the royal ſtandard to New York: the phraſe, *'tis all the ſame in Dutch*, being a local expreſſion ariſing from the numbers of German ſettlers in Pennſylvania. To the firſt two lines of the burthen the author gives a variation:

> Let old Diogenes ſettle the nation;
> He ne'er had a drop of good wine in his tub.

Note 35, Page 36.

The alluſion to the Howes in this verſe is ſufficiently clear. The capture of Burgoyne's army at Saratoga, and his dinner with General Gates, is alſo referred to.

Note 36, Page 36.

It was frequently declared, at this period, by the advocates of England, that Congreſs had given ſecretly ſome ſort of a lien upon part of the American territories to France, as a ſecurity for the aſſiſtance afforded us by that power. Of courſe there was no truth in the report. The exultations of the Americans, and of Congreſs in particular, was however (and naturally ſo) very great, at the proſpect of the reſults to flow from ſuch a connexion as the confederation had now formed. The firſt anniverſary of the day on which the Treaty was ſigned was celebrated by a banquet given by Congreſs to the French Miniſter; at which the King and Queen of France, the King of Spain, and all the Princes of the Houſe of Bourbon, were formally toaſted, under ſalvos of artillery. On the

the 8th of May, 1778, Congrefs had iffued an addrefs to the people, in which the certainty of victory over England was proclaimed, and a warm picture given of the profperity which would then attend the deftinies of the United States.

Note 37, Page 39.

Nothing more vigourous than *The Town Meeting* is to be found among all the loyal fatires produced during the revolutionary war; nor was its popularity furpaffed by that of any other of its clafs. That it hit the whigs feverely, and that its perfonalities were fhrewdly aimed, is evident to any one familiar with the hiftory of the times: and Stanfbury's familiarity with the people and politics of Philadelphia enabled him to eafily bring into fucceffful ridicule many of thofe fubordinate characters of the drama—*Glaucumque, Medontaque, Therfilochumque*—who rarely figure in ifolated pofitions on the pages of hiftory. The refult has been ftated in an earlier Note; the refentment of this clafs fubfifted in ftrength fufficient to prevent his return to the city after the Peace, while that of more important characters had long faded away. Men who are unaccuftomed to public admiration are generally unforgiving of public cenfure, or farcafm.

Unlike the majority of the author's productions that have appeared in this volume, *The Town Meeting* is not printed from his original manufcript. But as it was firft publifhed under his own infpection, that text has been taken as a ftandard for comparifon with a number of contemporaneous manufcript copies in various hands. One of thefe, formerly among the papers of the late Edward Duffield of Moreland, was printed feveral years fince, in an edition of ten copies, by the late Edward D. Ingraham; viz: The Town Meeting: A Tory Squib. From the Copy found among the Papers of the late Edward Duffield, Efquire, of Moreland. Le bon vieux temps. Philadelphia, 1837. 8 vo. pp. 8.

Another, though a flightly incorrect verfion is given in Watfon's Annals of Philadelphia, II; 204.

To properly comprehend the verfes, the condition of affairs exifting in
the

the city at the period muſt be preſent to the reader. The new conſtitution of Pennſylvania, adopted in 1776, was bitterly oppoſed by the moderate whigs, and alſo by almoſt every one who was not an active whig. It was ſupported in great meaſure by what John Adams called " the democratic " party." That it was firſt conceived or put forward to gratify the deſires of the wealthier and graver claſſes of the population is improbable. There were whiſpers that it was the fruit of the promptings of certain New England delegates in Congreſs, who were diſſatiſfied with any line likely to be purſued by an Aſſembly choſen excluſively by electors with a freehold qualification; and who therefore deviſed theſe means of procuring an alteration in the character of the provincial legiſlature. If there was any truth in this ſuggeſtion, John Adams could not have been involved in the buſineſs, for he had no good opinion of the new frame of government. His colleague Samuel Adams, however, intrigued ſo keenly to ſaddle it on a community of which he was not a citizen, as to provoke, according to Gordon, ſome perſons " to drop diſtant hints of an aſſaſſination." Once in operation, its power was wielded excluſively by the people that had procured its adoption; and if ſome, who at firſt decried its ſuitability to the wants and the rights of the inhabitants, afterwards became its expounders, it was becauſe there was no other means of obtaining civil authority in the State than by the aid of the new party.

In the mean time, the financial condition of the country was producing an effect on the minds of men. Up to 1779, there had been emitted, by Congreſs, about ſixty millions of dollars in paper money, which was then in circulation and unredeemed. There was alſo due by the United States, for moneys borrowed, about forty millions more. The terms of the articles of confederation gave Congreſs no ſufficient power to raiſe the means of diſcharging theſe debts : indeed, all the ſtates, though repreſented in that body, had not as yet conſented to the Confederation. At the period in queſtion, the Continental Treaſury had received in all but about three millions of dollars for taxes. It is therefore very plain that the Continental Paper Money could have had no other commercial value than what
aroſe

arofe from the common confent to give and take it in fome proportion or other to its nominal value.   Tender laws, which compelled creditors to ` receive it, or have their debts cancelled by refufal, ferved only to injure a certain number of mortgagees or bondholders ; they could not endow the paper money with vitality.   Nothing of courfe could do this but a reafonable ground of belief in its eventual redemption by the United States ; and the practical comment upon the juftice of fuch a belief may be feen in the bufhels of bills that cumbered, within the recollection of the prefent generation, more than one old garret.   Accordingly, the value of the notes iffued by Congrefs was daily decreafing through all the war : fo that while in 1780 three hundred pounds in this currency would buy a dog, and three thoufand an ox and a half and a few eggs ; in 1781, feven hundred pounds in paper reprefented but ten in fpecie ; and a mob is faid to have paraded through the ftreets of Philadelphia with colors flying and cock- ades of paper dollars in their hats, efcorting a dog which had been tarred and then ftuck over, not with feathers, but with congreffional paper money. In the next year this currency found its real value, at which it has re- mained ever fince.

The compulfory laws, which forced creditors to receive this money, could have produced no good effect on the morals of the community. Watfon obferves that one of the worft ufes to which it was put " was to " prefent it as ' a legal tender,' to pay with almoft no value what had been " before purchafed for a *bona fide* valuable confideration.   Many bafe men " fo acquired their property : efpecially when ' to cheat a tory ' was deemed " fair prize with feveral.   Houfes ftill ftand in Philadelphia, which, could " their walls fpeak out, would tell of ftrangely inconfiderable values re- " ceived for them by the fellers.   The large double houfe,. for inftance, " at the north-weft corner of Second and Pine ftreets, was once purchafed, " it was faid, with the money received for one hogshead of rum.   The " lot in Front, below Pine, whereon four or five large houfes ftood, called · " Barclay's Row, was fold for £60 only of real value."   When however the continued depreciation of the bills had reached a point that rendered

their

their own poſſeſſions unſafe, the whigs generally began to be uneaſy. Day by day its value decreaſed with the increaſe of its amount. A man might ſell a barrel of flour for a hundred pounds today, and tomorrow it would coſt him, to repurchaſe it, a hundred and twenty. Naturally, the prices of all ſorts of commodities were regulated by the value of the money with which they were to be bought. The ſmall dealers, who to a great extent ſold their own produce, were juſt as careful to follow the ſcale of depreciation as the extenſive merchant whoſe warehouſes were filled with goods. But as the latter very often ſought to obtain the control of the market by ſecuring, for the time being, the command of the ſupply, he was conſtantly liable to fall within the category of foreſtallers and monopoliſts. To prevent, therefore, the depreciation of the money, the authorities of the day contemplated the limitation of prices; while the government of Pennſylvania, in January, 1779, declared its intention of enforcing the heavieſt penalties againſt foreſtallers. Unfortunately, however, there would appear to have been ſuch a ſpice of partizan politics infuſed into the conſideration of this branch of the queſtion as to give room to ſuppoſe at the time that private as well as public motives would enter into the enforcement of theſe penalties. Robert Morris was then held in great diſlike by the party in the commonwealth that he was oppoſed to; and he was alſo the principal holder of flour among the merchants. He had, at this period, a contraẟ for procuring large quantities of that article for the French fleet. In furtherance of their objeẟs, a town meeting was held at Philadelphia on the 25th of May, 1779. The popular excitement, already ſufficiently great, was ſtimulated to fever heat by a parade of the militia on the day previous, as narrated by the poet in Canto Firſt: the proceedings of the meeting itſelf are in a meaſure told in Canto Second. But as it may not be amiſs to give a conneẟed account of the concluſion as well as of the beginning of this buſineſs, this Note will be carried to a greater length. I have before me a broadſide account of the occaſion, evidently publiſhed by authority of the officers of the day for the information of the public. The Chairman, General Roberdeau, after a ſpeech

In

in which the evils of foreftalling were dwelt upon; the orator's conviction declared that a combination had been formed for raifing the prices of
goods and provifions; the neceffity of fuch combinations being put down
by the people afferted; and the faĉt expatiated on, that during the paft
fix months prices had rifen week by week: then introduced a feries of
refolutions that had been prepared beforehand by a committee of citizens.
Thefe pointed out Robert Morris by name as the oftenfible aĉtor in
bringing about the recent rife of prices, and ordered that a committee
fhould inveftigate his conduĉt, and that he fhould anfwer in writing the
interrogatories to be put to him: that the prices of Weft India goods, tea,
flour, &c., fhould inftantly be reduced to the rates of May 1ft; that
offenders againft thefe refolutions fhould be noticed by the committee;
that the conduĉt of fufpeĉted public officers under Congrefs be examined
into by another committee; that all perfons "inimical to the intereft and
"independence of the United States" fhould be expelled from the community, &c. Thefe refolutions were, after fome debate, agreed to.
On the next day (May 26th), General Jofeph Reed, Mr. Bayard, and
fome others, prefented a memorial to Congrefs on the fame fubjeĉts as had
occafioned the meeting: it was referred to a committee of which John
Dickinfon was chairman; and an anfwer prefently appeared that was not
at all fatiffaĉtory to thofe who prefented the memorial. On the 26th of
May, the Committee appointed at the Town Meeting on the 25th, publifhed a tariff of prices; at which rates only were people to be permitted
to buy and fell. In June, another and a yet lower tariff was adopted,
and the Committee made its power felt by feveral of the chief merchants,
whofe conduĉt had not tallied with the will of the people. Morris in
efpecial was the fubjeĉt of indignation. His own ftatement of his pofition,
and of the difturbances to which his bufinefs had been fubjeĉted, will be
found in the local newfpapers of the day. On the 26th July, the Committee, through William Bradford, Efq., its chairman, publifhed an Addrefs, in which the juftice and expediency of their conduĉt was maintained,
and the faĉt declared that the refult of the Town Meeting in May had
been

been to put a ſtop to the depreciation of paper money. The remonſtrance of eighty merchants who avowed, in the opening of their repreſentation, that ſince the days of the Stamp Act they had been ſteady and decided whigs, was publiſhed about the ſame time. It was more reaſonable than the Addreſs of the Committee, but it produced leſs effect. It was in vain that they urged that they had to contend, in making their purchaſes, with the ſame depreciation that their cuſtomers were aggrieved by : that a veſſel, for inſtance, ſuch as formerly could be bought for £600 or £700, now coſt upwards of £40,000. A conſiderable portion of the inhabitants were reſolute to ſuſtain the Committee, and would not be convinced by anything that could be ſaid by men whom party rage confounded with concealed Tories. In the end of June, a militia company of artillery declared its deſire to take up arms againſt their fellow-citizens in ſupport of the decrees of the Town Meeting and the Committee; and through the ſummer, the illwill and excitement was conſtantly on the increaſe. Morris, McClenachan, and other prominent characters were openly menaced, and placards were poſted, on the morning of October 4th, threatening the breaking open of their ſtores. A meeting of the Militia was called for that morning, the object of which was undoubtedly violence; and the mob, including a number of armed militia-men, took up their line of march through the city. It is not known now what particular end they had in view : but probably their intent was to act, as circumſtances might ſuggeſt, againſt all obnoxious perſons. They had already ſeized two ſuch individuals, when they arrived at the dwelling of James Wilſon, at the corner of Walnut and Third Streets. Wilſon was a whig, and a Signer of the Declaration of Independence; but he was of the ſame political creed as Robert Morris; and was additionally odious to the government party by reaſon of his ſervices as a lawyer, to a number of perſons not long before indicted for High Treaſon. He was therefore among thoſe threatened with popular vengeance; and ſome thirty or forty of his friends had aſſembled at his houſe to defend him. It would ſeem that this party compriſed ſeveral who were marked by the mob. Very happily, however,

ever, General Mifflin was one of the number, who was a warm political enemy of General Reed, the head of the executive of the ſtate. Mifflin had very ſagaciouſly adviſed that information of the approaching aſſault ſhould be ſent to General Reed, and his counſel had been carried into effect. The houſe being preſently attacked, and life loſt upon either ſide, Mifflin threw open a window, and attempted to addreſs the mob. A man immediately diſcharged his piece at him, the ball ſtriking the window-ſaſh cloſe by his body; on which the General returned the fire with both his piſtols. A byſtander relates that he queſtioned the aſſailant if he knew whoſe life he had aimed at: "he replied 'he ſuppoſed ſome damned "Tory,' and when I informed him that it was General Mifflin, he ex-"preſſed his ſurpriſe and regret." The mob, however, was repulſed, and for the moment retired. It preſently returned with cannon; and a party of men armed with ſledge-hammers and iron bars ſoon made a breach in the houſe. The arrival of General Reed with a couple of Baylor's dragoons, cauſed the aſſailants to pauſe; and very ſoon after a few of the Firſt City Troop charging into the crowd, it was completely diſperſed. The defenders of the houſe then ſallied out, and aided in the ſeizure of priſoners.

It is ſtated by Watſon that, in anticipation of the affray, the Troop (which was then as now compoſed of the gentry of the neighborhood) had prepared on this day to be ready for ſervice at a moment's warning. The deceitful calm that prevailed during the morning had induced the members to retire for dinner to their reſpective homes, and it was only nine of their number who were got together in time to act. Charging ſuddenly on the mob, ignorance of their real ſtrength aided the panic of their adverſaries; and the cry of "*the horſe, the horſe!*" was a ſignal for general flight. The party incurred great odium by this feat, and Major Lenox "was particularly marked out for deſtruction." His houſe at Germantown was ſubſequently ſurrounded in the night-time, and nothing but the opportune arrival of the Troop diſperſed his enemies. In alluſion to his having thrown aſide his long coat, to avoid being dragged from his horſe

on

on the 4th of October, and thus riding into action in his ſhirt-ſleeves, he was for years after accoſted as "brother butcher" in the market-place. Watſon alſo gives the names of ſome of the defenders of the houſe:

"Meſſrs. Wilſon, Morris, Burd, George and Daniel Clymer, John T. "Mifflin, Allen McLane, Sharpe Delaney, George Campbell, Paul Beck, "Thomas Laurence, Andrew Robinſon, John Potts, Samuel C. Morris, "Captain Campbell, and Generals Mifflin, Nichols, and Thompſon. "They were provided with arms, but their ſtock of ammunition was "very ſmall. While the mob was marching down, General Nichols and "Daniel Clymer proceeded haſtily to the Arſenal at Carpenter's Hall, and "filled their pockets with cartridges: this conſtituted their ſole ſupply. "* * * Allen McLane and Colonel Grayſon got into the houſe after the "fray began. The mob called themſelves *Conſtitutionaliſts*. Benezet's "fire in the entry from the cellar paſſage was very effective." John Schaffer, and Colonel Chambers of Lancaſter, were alſo in the houſe. Captain Campbell was killed: he had ſerved in Hazen's Continental Regiment and had loſt an arm. Indeed moſt of the defenders ſeem to have been connected with the Continental Army, while their opponents were chiefly of the Militia. Such of the latter as had been arreſted after their repulſe, were ſent to gaol. On the next day, the Militia Officers aſſembled, and there were apprehenſions that they would enforce the releaſe of their comrades. The matter ended by the priſoners being diſcharged on bail; and the party in the houſe were alſo compelled to enter into recognizances. No other legal proceedings were taken by the government of the State, ſave an act of general pardon to all concerned in the affair, whereby both ſides eſcaped without trial and without puniſhment.

This tragic concluſion terminated the ſcene which had occupied the public ſtage ſince the 25th of May; and the oppoſite parties amongſt the whigs were thenceforth more tranquil in their hoſtility. It is noticeable, however, that the flame kindled during 1779 never entirely burned out ſo long as ſome of thoſe who ſhared in the excitement ſurvived. It was the

belief

belief of more than one of his enemies that General Reed was implicated in the deſign of the riot: but the charge is not ſupported. Watſon remarks that General Arnold came to repreſs the mob, but he was ſo unpopular that they ſtoned him. Arnold was Reed's open enemy. He arrived with his weapons at Wilſon's houſe juſt after the riot was quelled, and turning to the byſtanders, obſerved: " Your Preſident has raiſed a " mob, and now he cannot quell it." Reed was ill in bed when the riot occurred ; and ſeveral years after, in reference to the remark that he had gone to quell it at the riſk of his life, I find this ſtatement in the manuſcript of a Philadelphian who certainly bore him no good will: " That is true: " for, as he had raiſed the mob, it was inſiſted he ſhould go out and " and quiet them, and his life was threatened if he did not."

The ſeventeenth and eighteenth Stanzas of the Second Canto of *The Town Meeting* are quoted in the Life and Correſpondence of Preſident Reed, volume 2nd, page 149 : which ſhows that Stanſbury's ſatiric ſhafts did not, in every inſtance, penetrate very deeply.

For other particulars of this criſis in the revolutionary hiſtory of Pennſylvania, which for a moment ſo nearly threatened the inauguration of ſcenes ſuch as thoſe that a few years later tranſpired in France, ſee *Reed's Reed*, II; *c.* 6: *Biog. Signers*, VI;. 150. The local newſpapers of the day appear to have refrained from the ſlighteſt alluſion to the *emeute*.

Note 38, Page 39.

Watſon makes this ſtanza refer to General Reed, but he is in error, it would ſeem. " John Bayard, for a time Speaker of the Pennſylvania " Aſſembly, and a Major in the regiment of which Mr. Roberdeau was " Colonel and Mr. Reed Lieutenant-Colonel " is believed to be the perſon alluded to. As early as 1774, Mr. Bayard was an active whig in the politics of High Street Ward, Philadelphia. Early in 1776 he and Roberdeau fitted out a privateer which ſoon captured a valuable prize. In 1785 he was a member of Congreſs, and died in 1807. His nephew, James A. Bayard, was one of the American negotiators at Ghent, and

his

his great-nephews are alſo diſtinguiſhed in the public ſervice. *To ſave one's bacon* is an Americaniſm, then as now in vogue: "A ſuperior "ſquadron of our allies may come upon the coaſt in time to ſave our "bacon; there I confeſs I reſt my almoſt only hope."—*Gates to Reed,* 10th May, 1780.

Note 39, Page 40.

Blair M'Clenachan was a leading merchant in Philadelphia, and an active whig. A New York letter of April 19th, 1780, ſays: "Yeſter-"day arrived in our harbour the brigantine *Macaroni*, commanded by "—— Patterſon, belonging to Mr. Blair M'Lanachan, of Philadelphia. "She mounts 14 guns, is a perfect beauty, and was taken by his Majeſty's "ſhip Delight, Captain Inglis." In June of the ſame year, he ſubſcribed £10,000 to the eſtabliſhment of the Bank of Pennſylvania, of which he was choſen Inſpector with Robert Morris, and three more. Morris ſub-ſcribed a like ſum. The object of this inſtitution was to facilitate the obtaining ſupplies for the army. Of other characters referred to in *The Town Meeting*, it may be added here that Joſeph Reed ſubſcribed £2000; Thomas M'Kean, John Mitchell, and Benjamin Ruſh, £2000 each; and Michael Hillegas, £4000: by which it appears that the friends and foes of 1779 were willing to unite for the good of the country in 1780. In 1782, it has been ſaid that he loſt heavily, by engaging in a ſort of licenſed gambling, cuſtomary in former times. An account was publiſhed, in Rivington's (New York) Gazette, of Rodney's victory over the Count de Graſſe, and of the capture of the *Ville de Paris*, the French Admiral's flag-ſhip. Rivington's paper was of ſo little credit with the whigs, that none of them believed the ſtory: and they were confirmed in their opinions by the arrival of an American privateer whoſe people had wit-neſſed the commencement only of the engagement; but whoſe account of what they ſaw varied widely from Rivington's ſtatement. In addition the *Ville de Paris* was ſo large and powerful a ſhip that the officers of a French veſſel, captured by the Engliſh ſome time after, being informed

of

of the reſult of the engagement, were exceedingly downcaſt until they were told of the flagſhip's misfortune: on which their ſpirits immediately revived :—" it was all a miſtake, a deluſion," they cried ;—" the *Ville de* " *Paris* could not poſſibly be taken." But William Bingham, Eſq., who had means of obtaining very good intelligence from the Weſt' Indies, had probably received ſecret but authentic tidings : at leaſt it was ſo reported at Philadelphia ſoon after. He therefore commenced to open policies on the ſafety of the *Ville de Paris* with all who would underwrite her. Theſe were chiefly the warm and wealthy whigs, and M'Clenachan is ſaid to have been of the number. Bingham and his friends paid at firſt 10 *per cent* premium, and from that up to 25 and 30 *per cent.* Some four or five hundred thouſand dollars were thus underwritten. The one ſide was encouraged in its miſtake by a letter received by the French Miniſter, written from Martinico after the battle, that gave cauſe to believe the *Ville de Paris* had not been taken ; while the other relied on its own intelligence, whatever that might have been. After the war, M'Clenachan was ſued in England by one *Brag* for damages cauſed by him while acting under public authority from the Americans. This proceeding, however unjuſt in itſelf, was balanced by the New York Statute of 17th March, 1783, preſcribing ſimilar meaſures againſt the other ſide. He finally failed in buſineſs, and was impriſoned for debt. He was a warm anti-federaliſt: his propoſition at a public meeting during Waſhington's adminiſtration, ' to kick Jay's Treaty to hell ' excited much merriment at the time. He ſeems to have been a warmhearted, enthuſiaſtic man, and a liberal friend to the American cauſe during the war.

Note 40, Page 40.

Art. IV. " That all power being originally inherent in, and conſe-quently derived from, the people ; therefore all officers of government, whether legiſlative or executive, are their truſtees and ſervants, and at all times accountable to them."—*Pennſylvania Conſtitution of* 1776: *Chap. i.*

NOTE

Note 41, Page 40.

Robert Morris, Benedict Arnold, and (according to a manuſcript note) William Wiſtar, are here referred to. The firſt was as diſtinguiſhed for his abilities as a financier, as the ſecond for his reckleſs and perſevering courage as a ſoldier. This was while he was ſtationed at Philadelphia, and before his treaſon. Wiſtar was perhaps a citizen of Germantown.

Note 42, Page 40.

"Benjamin Paſchall, Eſquire; Juſtice of the Peace, and Shoemaker." —*Author's Note.*

Note 43, Page 40.

The green ſprig of foliage ſometimes worn in the hat by the Americans, in lieu of a cockade.

Note 44, Page 41.

If the barber who ſhaved John Adams, and who figures ſo amuſingly in Adams's letters to his wife of 23rd April, 1776, and 28th March, and 23rd April, 1777, was a fair type of their politics, the barbers of Philadelphia muſt have been ſtaunch whigs. Adams deſcribes him as a dapper little fellow, with an untiring tongue; a ſergeant in one of the militia battalions; and troubled with remorſe at miſſing his chance of fortune in the *Rattleſnake* privateer, which with the *Sturdy Beggar*, had taken eleven fine prizes. "Confound the ill luck, Sir; I was going to ſea my-" "ſelf on board the *Rattleſnake,* and my wife fell a yelping. Theſe wives" "are queer things. I told her I wondered ſhe had no more ambition." "'Now,' ſays I, 'when you walk the ſtreets and any body aſks who that" "is? The anſwer is *Burne the barber's wife.* Should you not be better" "pleaſed to hear it ſaid, *That is Captain Burne's lady,* the Captain of" "marines on board the *Rattleſnake?*' 'O,' ſays ſhe, 'I would rather" "be

" called Burne the barber's wife, than Captain Burne's widow. I don't
" defire to live better than you maintain me, my dear.' So it is, Sir, by
" this fweet, honey language, I am choufed out of my prizes, and muft
" go on with my foap and razors and pincers and combs. I wifh fhe
" had my ambition."

Note 45, Page 41.

A manufcript note fupplies here the name of a perfon " whipp'd at
" Annapolis : now a Committee-man."

Note 46, Page 41.

" Dr. Fallon, chairman of one of the Committees."—*Manufcript Note.*

Note 47, Page 41.

One manufcript of *The Town Meeting* has *Porter Mich.* and adds this
note to the whole line : " The one a Porter, the other a Fifherman ; now
" Captains in the Army." Watfon alfo reads Mich.; and the verfion
printed from the Duffield copy fays *Pewterer* Will. I prefer to follow
the text in Rivington. *Mich.* might poffibly refer to Michael Hillegas,
a whig of confiderable local influence ; but the defcription of his antecedents will not apply. *Will* may fignify Colonel Will, afterwards Sheriff
of Philadelphia County.

Note 48, Page 41.

" John Mitchell, famous for eating Shad-roe," fays a note in the Duffield impreffion. He is referred to in the third Stanzas of this Canto.
In 1777, Colonel Mitchell was Adjutant-General of Pennfylvania. The
Marquis de Chaftellux in a fketch of one of the City Affembly Balls at
Philadelphia in the winter of 1780-1 (where the airs danced to, by the
way, went by the names of *Burgoyne's Defeat, The Succefs of the Campaign, Clinton's Retreat,* &c.) fays : " The Managers are generally chofen
" from

" from amongst the most distinguished officers of the Army ; this import-
" ant place is at present held by Colonel *Wilkinson*, who is also a clothier-
" general of the Army.   Colonel *Mitchell*, a little fat, squat man, fifty
" years old, a great judge of horses, and who was lately Contractor for
" carriages, both for the American and the French Armies, was formerly
" the Manager ; but when I saw him, he had descended from the magis-
" tracy, and danced like a private citizen.   He is said to have exercised
" his office with great severity, and it is told of him, that a young lady
" who was figuring in a Country Dance, having forgot her turn by con-
" versing with a friend, he came up to her, and called out aloud, *give over,*
" *Miss, take care what you are about : Do you think you came here for*
" *your pleasure ?*"

Note 49, Page 41.

Thomas M'Kean ; a Member of the Congress of 1765, a Signer of the
Declaration ; and the only man who was constantly a Member of Congress from 1774 to 1783.   He was President of Congress in 1781 ;
Chief-Justice ; and Governor of Pennsylvania.   He may have dressed in
black, as described by the poet, in private life : but on the bench he was
distinguished by his immense cocked-hat and scarlet gown.   He died in
1817, in his 84th year.

Note 50, Page 41.

Continental Paper Money.

Note 51, Page 42.

Timothy Matlack : in 1780 a Member of Congress from Pennsylvania.

Note

NOTE 52, Page 42.

Colonel John Bull of Philadelphia county; afterwards of Montgomery county. In 1772, he was a Juftice of the Peace; in 1777, he was Colonel of the Firft Regiment of Pennfylvania Levies; and a Member of Affembly from Philadelphia County. He commanded at Billingfport; and was Adjutant General of the Militia.

NOTE 53, Page 42.

" Daniel Roberdeau, a lumber merchant and militia general."—*Manu-fcript Note.* A Member of Congrefs with Robert Morris from Pennfylvania in 1777; and that body meeting at York, where accommodations were fcanty, he opened his houfe to Gerry, and Samuel and John Adams, delegates from Maffachufetts. Though of French extraction, he was a great public favourite at Philadelphia, where he had long dwelt. The following Warrant, iffued (if genuine) when the Whigs there were preparing to fly before the enemy, is not printed in the Archives.—" *In* " *Council of Safety*, Philadelphia, Dec. 9, 1776. You are hereby au-" thorized and required to imprefs either *James Pemberton's, John Pem-* " *berton's, Samuel Emlen's,* jun., or *John Reynolds'* clofe carriage and " horfes, for to remove General Roberdeau. By Order of Council. " *David Rittenhoufe, V. Prefident.* To John Bray, or any other Con-" ftable." Thefe coach owners were probably not very zealous whigs. Roberdeau's education muft have been good. In 1777, we find him writing to feveral of the State Authorities, afking that copies of Virgil and of Ovid fhould be fent him; which might have occafioned the fatirift, who reflected that the legiflature of 1778 could not all write their own names, to repeat how often it happened that " the moft capricious poet, " honeft Ovid, was among the Goths." In January, 1795, Adams writes: " The public prints announce the death of my old, efteemed friend, " General Roberdeau, whofe virtues in heart-fearching times endeared

" him

" him to Philadelphia and to his country. His friendly attention to me
" when Congreſs held their ſeſſions at Yorktown I can never forget," &c.
He is buried at Alexandria.

NOTE 54, Page 42.

Goſhen is not remote from New York; which city, being the Britiſh
headquarters, is here ſignified. The expulſion of the wives and children
of Tories was not, in ſo many words, included in the Reſolutions of the
Town Meeting of May 25th: but the preſence in the city of the wives
of " Britiſh Emiſſaries " was preſented as " a grievance of a very danger-
" ous nature " by the Grand Jury, in July, 1779: and in June, 1780,
the Executive Council of the State ordered that the wives and children
of all perſons who had joined the Enemy, if found within the State after
the lapſe of ten days from the date of that Decree, ſhould be proceeded
againſt as public enemies.

NOTE 55, Page 43.

" The mob are not eaſily pleaſ'd. While General Roberdeau was
ſpeaking from the chair, thoſe behind him hiſſ'd and ſilenc'd him, becauſe he turn'd his face from them."—*Author's Note.*

NOTE 56, Page 43.

Dr. James Hutchinſon: born 1752; died of yellow fever, 1793. He
was by birth a Quaker. See his biography in *Reed's Reed,* 11; 127;
and a free notice of his character in *Littell's Graydon,* 91. John Adams
too muſt have diſliked him exceſſively, when he repeated what ſome
Quakers in Philadelphia had told him of the benefits to the United States
that reſulted from Hutchinſon's death.

NOTE 57, Page 43.

" A gander has more brains by half:" and " A gooſe has got more
" ſenſe by half;" are other readings of this line.

NOTE

Note 58, Page 43.

Dr. Benjamin Rush : but the adjective does not agree with Mr. Adams's estimate, in 1775, of Rush's character. " He is an elegant, ingenious " body, a sprightly, pretty fellow. He is a republican. * * * But Rush, " I think, is too much of a talker to be a deep thinker ; elegant, not " great."—*Life and Works*, 11; 427. From circumstances, and his own talents, few men became more odious to the Tories than Rush : and he cordially reciprocated their sentiments. Smyth, who while in gaol at Philadelphia came into contact with him, styles him " a man eminent in " physic, but as eminent in rebellion, and still more so in unfulfilled pro- " fessions." But every thing that envy, hatred, malice, and all uncharita- bleness, ever did to vilify the character, conduct and connexions of Dr. Rush, pales beside the rancorous hatred and the powerful idiom of Cob- bett, who actually kept up a periodical called *The Rush-Light*, with no other end or staple than witty abuse of the doctor and his friends : its motto was from *Job :*—" Can the rush grow up without mire ? can the " flag grow without water ? Whilst it is yet in his greenness, and not cut " down, it withereth before any other herb. So are the paths of all that " forget God ; and the hypocrite's hope shall perish," &c. See *Porcu- pine's Works*, xii : *Index*.

Note 59, Page 43.

" Timothy Matlack, Esq., called from his cock-fighting propensities, " *Tim Gaff*."—*Duffield*.

Note 60, Page 43.

George Bryan, Esq. ; born in Ireland, 1730; died in Pennsylvania, 27th January, 1791. He was prominent as a leader of the democratic wing of the Whig Party. See a previous Note: also *Reed's Reed*, 11: *Index ;* and *Littell's Graydon*, 287. " He was said to be a very diligent reader, " and

" and was certainly a never weary monotonous talker, who, in the dif-
" courses he held, seldom failed to give evidence of the most minute, re-
" condite, and out of the way facts; insomuch, that a bet was once offered,
" that he could name the town-cryer of Bergen-op-Zoom."

Note 61, Page 44.

Alluding to the bribe alleged to have been tendered by Commodore
Johnstone to General Reed; and refused: a matter that was the source
of much comment on both sides of the Atlantic. The three persons involved; Johnstone, who offered the bribe; Mrs. Ferguson, who bore the
message; and Reed, who repulsed it; had each a different version of the
affair. Mrs. Ferguson admitting the truth of Reed's account, so far as
he and Johnstone were concerned, at the same time denied that he had
stated his conversation with her in either a fair, friendly, or kind manner.
Johnstone declared there was not a word of truth in the whole story, and
asserted that he had indisputable evidence in his possession to show that
Reed's story was untrue. This evidence, he continued, could not be
made public at the time, lest it should endanger the safety of private individuals; but he intimated that it should one day be given to the world.
Its nature never has been made known: and there is little doubt but that
the narratives of Reed and Mrs. Ferguson were substantially correct.
Johnstone indeed admits that he used corrupt means in other instances;
as truly there was reason to believe would have been attempted. Arthur
Lee wrote from Paris to Congress in 1778, when Carlisle, Eden, and
Johnstone were about setting forth as Royal Commissioners to America,
that " the ministers of England give out that they have despatched half a
" million of guineas, to pave the way to a favourable reception of their pro-
" positions, and I know from the best authority here that they have assured
" Count Maurepas of their being *sure of a majority in Congress.*" Lee
was an enemy of Reed's,—(the same calumniator, wrote Franklin to
Reed in 1780, " who formerly, in his private letters to particular mem-
" bers, accused you, with Messrs. Jay, Duane, Langdon, and Harrison,

" of

" of betraying the ſecrets of Congreſs, in a correſpondence with the Miniſ-
" try:")—and his teſtimony therefore as to the unworthy artifices to be
employed, is of importance. A writer in Hall and Sellers' Gazette (Philadelphia, September 1ſt, 1779), remarks with great earneſtneſs on Johnſtone's
general avowal of the uſe of " other means beſides perſuaſion." He declares
it to be the opinion " of many hardy zealots in our cauſe," reaſoning from
the conduct of the Congreſs of 1778-9, that " it is impoſſible that General
" Reed, whoſe conſequence in Congreſs was not of the firſt order, could
" be the only member of that body who did not attract the notice of a
" bribe.   To this great and good man a bribe was undeniably offered.
" It was no doubt offered to others.   Gen. Reed was the only one who
" divulged, and therefore the only one who refuſed it—for if offered to
" others, and that it muſt have been offered to others beſides the General,
" is next to a certainty, how came it to paſs (ſay theſe ſcrutinizing zealots)
" that they did not, like him, for reputation ſake even, divulge the pro-
" ferred corruption?"   If this inſinuation had any real foundation, I
cannot explain it: but if, as is moſt likely, it was deſigned to affect the
political antagoniſts of the local party to which Reed belonged, its explanation may conſiſt in the facts already referred to in the Notes to *The
Town Meeting*, of the hatred in which Robert Morris was then held by
many; Mr. Morris, Mr. Dana, and Mr. Reed having each been addreſſed,
on his arrival, by letters from Johnſtone.   Governeur Morris and William
Duer, Members of Congreſs from New York, were alſo, in 1779, on
terms of political hoſtility with General Reed.

Note 62, Page 44.

" *Vide the Letter from* Cleves *on the Lower Rhine*, in Dunlap's Penn-
" ſylvania Packet, May 25th, 1779."—*Author's Note*.   " Alluding to a
" piece publiſhed in the ſaid paper ſounding the good Qualifications of
" Preſident Reed: *ſtrongly ſuſpected to be compoſed by himſelf*."—*Manuſcript Note*.   This laſt inſinuation is probably falſe.   The article in queſtion was undoubtedly printed in Europe, and thence tranſlated to America,
Mr.

Mr. C. G. F. Dumas, the Private Agent in Holland for American Affairs, wrote (4th November, 1778) from the Hague to the American Commiſſioners at Paris in this wiſe :—" The Courier of the Lower Rhine " contains a fine eulogy on Mr. Joſeph Reed, member of Congreſs; it is " deſerving of your attention. I wiſh I could ſend you the paper, but " I have only one copy, which I am about to forward to Congreſs." The following is the letter (probably altered to an Engliſh dreſs) as it appeared in Dunlap's Packet of May 25th, 1779.

Extract from a Gazette, printed at Cleves, on the Lower Rhine.

" The noble and diſintereſted conduct of the members of the American Congreſs, whom the Britiſh Commiſſioners endeavored to corrupt, has been received here with equal pleaſure and admiration. They have generouſly diſdained the moſt ſeducing offers that were made, and have therefore given the lie to the aſſertion of an Agent from the Court of London to that of Verſailles, to a gentleman in high office.—' The end of this affair will prove that your nation has been the dupes of it. After you have made great efforts, and incurred immenſe expenſes, to ſupport American Independence, we ſhall purchaſe the Members of Congreſs, and the Congreſs itſelf: a little Gold diſtributed appropos will reëſtabliſh us in all our rights, and cover you with ſhame for your proceedings.'—I am not worth purchaſing, but ſuch as I am, the King of Great Britain is not· rich enough to do it! Virtuous and ſublime Reed! Do not believe that we can paſs over in ſilence a reply ſo magnanimous, ſo generous, worthy of being equalled to the fineſt expreſſions of patriotiſm and greatneſs of ſoul, of which the antient republics offer an example. Should this writing ever find its way to you, accept the homage which we pay to thy virtue, in the name of all thoſe whoſe hearts know the worth of it. May your example find many imitators in your country, where baſeneſs and venality have not made the fatal progreſs they have done in the countries of Europe! Such inſtances of magnanimity remind us that, four years ago, when the firſt ſteps towards independence were taken, we ventured to predict

' That

'That the Americans would exhibit examples of grandeur that would aftonifh our little fouls.' And we have every day the fatiffaction to fee that we have not miftaken this extraordinary people, made to do honour to human nature, and to recall the idea of its primitive dignity."

NOTE 63, Page 45.

The fleet under D'Eftaing was fent from France with a view to deftroy the Britifh fquadron in the Delaware, and thus lend a vital affiftance to the caufe of America.   Had it, inftead, failed directly to the Weft or Eaft Indies or to other expofed poffeffions of England, it might doubtlefs have gained great advantages for France.   The length of time D'Eftaing was on the voyage, and the tidings that came to the Englifh, enabled them to get on their guard; and the French on arrival found them gone to New York.   After landing M. Gerard, the Minifter, D'Eftaing proceeded to Sandy Hook, where for eleven days, in the fummer of 1778, he lay moored outfide the bar.   The pilots could not carry his largeft fhips over; and thus a fmaller fquadron, at New York under Howe, efcaped the dubious conflict.   The French admiral then went to Rhode Ifland, to coöperate with the American land forces under Sullivan againft the Britifh: where, after fome fkirmifhing he was overtaken by a ftorm; and his fleet fuffered much lofs ere he could get into Bofton.   His flag-fhip, the *Languedoc*, 90, loft her rudder and mafts.   The Americans were very angry at his leaving Newport and refufing to fend any of his veffels back from Bofton: and did not omit to publifh their vexation in protefts and general orders.   While refitting at Bofton (September, 1778), a ferious row occurred between his people and fome on the fhore. Whether the laft were Americans, or Britifh prifoners, I do not know: but one or two of the French officers were dangeroufly, if not mortally wounded.   A like occurrence was faid to have occurred at Charlefton, S. C., about the fame period; when the French from their fhips fired cannon and mufketry, which the Americans retorted from the wharves. After his fleet was refitted, D'Eftaing left Bofton, for Martinique as was

believed,

believed. The attempt at Newport, by the way, was a failure. The Americans were forced to retire when the French fleet no longer ſupported them.

Note 64, Page 45.

This is an early alluſion to Tamenund, the Indian king, as the patron ſaint of America.

Note 65, Page 47.

Rev. George Duffield, a chaplain to Congreſs, and a Preſbyterian. The alluſion, that follows, to the attendance of Congreſs, at a Catholic Maſs, refers to the willingneſs of that body, though Proteſtant, to pay a proper reſpect to the faith of the French King and of his Ambaſſador.

Note 66, Page 48.

We know that Odell was a French ſcholar; for in December, 1776, he acted as interpreter in that tongue between the Heſſian commander and the people of Burlington, N. J.: but he does great injuſtice here to the prowefs of the incomparable monarch of the Dipſodes, as deſcribed by Rabelais: who, after kicking the monſtrous Loupgarou to death, ſeized his corpſe by the two heels, and uſed it as a club to demoliſh the remainder of his enemies. " Finablement, voyant que tous eſtoyent mortz, " iecta le corps de Loupgarou tant qu'il peut contre la ville, et tumba " comme une grenouille ſûs le ventre en le place mage de ladicte ville, et " en tumbant du coup tua ung chat bruſle, une chatte mouillee, une canne " petiere, et ung oyſon bridé."—*La Vie de Gargantua et de Pantagruel:* liure ii. chap. xxix.

Note 67, Page 48.

Governor Samuel Huntington, of Connecticut, was Preſident of Congreſs, in 1779 and 1780. M. de Chaſtellux was reminded by him of Fabricius, when he paid the Preſident a viſit and found his chamber lit by a ſolitary candle, Note

Note 68, Page 50.

Charles-Hector, comte D'Eftaing, had ferved under Lally in India, and was captured at Madras by the Englifh in 1759. He broke his parole: wherefore, being again taken prifoner, the Englifh would not truft him, but lodged him in dureffe. This circumftance gave birth to his continued animofity to Britain. His French biographer accufes him of time-ferving in the civil turmoils of that kingdom: he teftified againft Marie Antoinette at her trial, and was prefently guillotined in his own turn. M. de la Mothe Piquet was another French naval officer of diftinction, who ferved on our coafts during the war.

Note 69, Page 50.

The Oneidas were the only tribe of the Six Nations in the intereft of Congrefs. In 1779, Gen. Sullivan (whofe objection to being left by D'Eftaing at Newport, in 1778, as already referred to, gives point to this allufion) led an expedition againft the hoftile favages, and exchanged fpeeches with the Oneidas. Unlefs I am miftaken, Congrefs beftowed military rank upon feveral of the chiefs of this tribe: an inexpenfive grant of honours, that probably fuggefted its repetition to the poet.

Note 70, Page 51.

The capture of the *Alcmene* frigate, October 21ft, 1779, gave Rear Admiral Hyde Parker the firft affurance of D'Eftaing being gone to America.

Note 71, Page 52.

D'Eftaing's firft fummons to Savannah was that it fhould furrender to the arms of the King of France. It may be noticed here, by the way, that the firft news of the defence of Savannah reached New York on the

18th

18th November, 1779, five days only before that on which *The Feu de Joie* appeared in print. This evinces a rapidity of compoſition on the part of Dr. Odell. His ſtory follows entirely the letters of Governor Tonyn and Colonel Fuſer, which contained the intelligence referred to.

Note 72, Page 53.

Captain Moncrieffe was an old ſoldier, and a good one. His extenſive acquaintance with this country, and the faƈt of his being the uncle of General Montgomery and the brother-in-law of Mr. Jay and Governor Livingſton, had inſpired a vain hope that he might adopt our cauſe. His ſervices as Engineer Officer at Savannah were, in great part, the ſalvation of the place; and General Prevoſt, in his official report, declared that any mark of royal favour beſtowed on Moncrieffe would be regarded as a perſonal gratification to every man in the army. He planned the works before Charleſton in the following year, and received Clinton's moſt profuſe praiſes in the Gazette. In a traƈt, publiſhed after the war, and written, it is ſuſpeƈted by Arnold, an anecdote is given of the battle of Brandywine. The Engliſh were advancing on the redoubt that Waſhington had thrown up to guard Chad's Ford, when Lieutenant Colonel (then Captain) Moncrieffe, who headed the column, ſaw an American howitzer, loaded with grape, pointed ſo as to rake the party, and the gunner about to apply the lighted match. " I'll put you to death if you fire!" Moncrieffe cried; on which the gunner dropped the match and fled. He died at New York, Dec. 10th, 1791; and was buried " in " Trinity Church, in the ſame tomb with his friend Colonel Maitland, " uncle to Lord Lauderdale, who, in dying, made it the laſt requeſt that " his aſhes ſhould be mixed with my father's." See *Memoirs of Mrs. Margaret Coghlan*, Moncrieffe's daughter, and a very notorious woman, who numbered the Duke of York among her keepers.

Note

Note 73, Page 53.

Colonel Maitland, an excellent officer, ſucceeded in getting into the town after the ſiege began. The relief he brought was very important, as the place, not expecting ſuch an attack, was not ſtrongly garriſoned. I have not ſeen this epitaph on him in print.

On the honourable Colonel Maitland, whoſe death was occaſioned by the fatigues he ſuffered in his admired march from Beaufort to Savannah, and whoſe memory in the Charles Town Gazette receives its higheſt panegyrick from the mouth of an enemy. *By Mrs. De Lancey.*

> O'er *Maitland's* corpſe as Victory reclin'd
> Reflecting on the fate of human kind :
> Is this, ſhe cried, the end of all thy toils !
> What now avail thy laurels or thy ſpoils !
>
> Worn with fatigue thou cam'ſt thy friends to ſave—
> Saw them reliev'd, and ſunk into the grave !
> Now grief and joy together blend their cries ;
> Savannah's ſav'd, yet generous Maitland dies.
> In vain around thy conq'ring ſoldiers weep :
> Thy eyes are cloſ'd in death's eternal ſleep.
> Yet while a grateful King or Country ſighs,
> O'er thy lov'd aſhes marbles proud ſhall riſe.
> Nay, even the Foe, reliev'd awhile from fear,
> Confeſs thy Virtues, and beſtow a tear :
> Own, that as Valour ſtrung thy nervous arm,
> So gentle Pity did thy boſom warm.
>
> O double praiſe—to make the haughty bend ;
> Yet make the vanquiſh'd enemy a friend !
> Thus *Maitland* falls, though his undying name
> Shall live forever on the lips of Fame.

Note

Note 74, Page 56.

Pulafki had been one of the Confederates of Bar to ouft Staniflaus Poniatowfki from the Polifh throne. Having fkilfully feized and carried off the king, he and his party do not feem to have known what to do with him : they had not the means of long retaining him prifoner, and they were not willing to flay him ; fo Staniflaus efcaped, and Pulafki fled the kingdom.

It is related, by one who was prefent, that in the moment of attack the advance on Savannah was delayed by the punctilio of an officer, whofe company had failed to obtain the pofition of honour upon the right, to which military etiquette entitled it. Under a fweeping fire of grapefhot from the town, the whole divifion was halted, while his company, with drum and fife, marched before the line to its place.

Note 75, Page 56.

This may refer to a fmall fortie on the night of Sept. 27th, which fet the French and Americans firing on each other in the dark. Their lofs was faid to be about fifty. When the fiege was about being given over, mutual civilities paffed between the Englifh and French officers, and one of the latter (Count O'Duin, an officer of rank) is reported by General Prevoft as fpeaking very acrimoniofly of " the fcoundrel Lincoln " and the Americans. General Benjamin Lincoln led our forces. Another Englifh Officer mentioned a report that the Americans were offended at the fummons to furrender to the French King only ; and that the allies when they departed " were almoft ready to cut one another's throats."

Note 76, Page 66.

Mariot Arbuthnot, nephew of Dr. John Arbuthnot the famous friend of Swift and Pope, was born in 1711, and died an Admiral of the Blue in 1794. In 1780, he commanded the naval forces at New York.
When

When the French fleet came to Rhode-Island in July, 1780, Clinton wished to make a conjoined attack on the enemy there, but the Admiral, who was not only a bad tactician but a flow old man, did not act with sufficient haste, and all fell through. In recruiting at New York, he dropped a coarse remark which is not repeated in the text as here reprinted. Sir Henry Clinton in a Manuscript Note says: " It had been " proposed that 6000 men under Sir H. C. should have been landed in " Escourt Passage to meet the French on their embarkation : but as the " Admiral was not informed of their arrival till ten days after, and that " they had been reinforced and had had time to fortify, it would not " have been quite so prudent for the Army alone to attempt; and if the " Admiral had seen the propriety of taking an active part with the " Navy, he would have accepted the proposal of Sir H. C."

Note 77, Page 72.

The King's floop *Savage*, of 16 guns, was loft near the river St. Lawrence before 1780: the *Triton* was a look-out veffel of Arbuthnot's fleet at New York in 1780.

Note 78, Page 72.

A place hard by New York where, it would appear, captive American Officers were often detained and boarded at two dollars a week. See *Littell's Graydon*: 245-255.

Note 79, Page 72.

Here is a confirmation of the affertion of the anonymous tranflator of Chaftellux. Immenfe quantities of Englifh, Spanifh, and Portuguefe gold coin were brought into America, during the war, at the coft of Great Britain: but " had all of them holes punched in them, or were otherwife " diminifhed at New York, before they were fuffered to pafs the lines ; " from whence they obtained the name of *Robertfons* in the *rebel* country ;
" but

" but the profits, if any, of that commander, on this new edition of the
" coin, remain a ſecret." Major-General James Robertſon was the laſt
Royal Governor of New York: his juriſdiction never extended beyond
the lines of the city.

Note 80, Page 74.

The manuſcript of this Ode bears alſo the following obſcure lines:
" Dear Y—. Your ſcrap of Intelligence made a Mother's Eye gliſten
" with delight and gratitude. Are not theſe feelings on theſe occaſions
" finer than their lordly Maſters. Your withering twig explains it in a
" moment. Well! I have executed all your commands, verbal and
" written, and now, feeling myſelf ſomewhat boulder after this full de-
" claration, let me requeſt the favor of you to put the above in a better
" dreſs than its own dad could invent or make for it: which will be doing
" as you would be done by. Benny will convince you I have not
" omitted ſending a line, and that will evince this propoſition that I am
" *wholly yours.* R. R. Tueſday morng."

Note 81, Page 79.

Freſh meats were ſo coſtly in New York during the war that the day
commemorated by the poet was worthy of all his praiſe. Taking the
prices for any year, we ſee how ſcarce freſh proviſions muſt have been.
In Feb. 1777, for inſtance, ſtrong Iriſh butter was at 3s. per lb. In
April, beef was at 14d. per lb.; butter at 2s.; mutton at 18d.; milk 7d.
per quart; cabbages 20d. each, &c. In June, an egg was worth a ſhil-
ling: in Auguſt, beef was at 21d. per lb., and other things in proportion.
The Song alſo refers to the cheriſhed idea with Waſhington and La Fayette of carrying New York. La Fayette was now in Virginia, acting
againſt Arnold.

NOTE

NOTE 82, Page 81.

The manufcript is addreffed : " To Capt. Duncan. P. P.'s correc-
" tion and alteration of the enclofed hafty dafh is requefted by the author."
Captain Duncan was of the *Eagle*, Lord Howe's flagfhip, in 1778. The
Royal Oak, 74, failed from England with " the hardy Byron " in 1778,
and was for feveral years in the American feas. M. Deftouches was at
Rhode-Ifland, in Auguft, 1780, in command of *Le Neptune*, 74.

NOTE 83, Page 83.

Now *Burke*, with his *Profpect*, no longer can charm ;
Nor Giants or Goblins the Nation alarm.—*Author's Variation.*

NOTE 84, Page 88.

To caft a flur on the character of Wafhington would, today, be the
act, if of an American, of a very filly or a very difhoneft man. The
latitude of party heats and perfonal rivalries permitted a lefs reftrained
conduct during his life-time. The Tories had furely fome excufe for
fpeaking bitterly of the only man by whom the American Armies could
have been led to Victory and Independence ; for the vanquifhed party
has in all times poffeffed at leaft the privilege of murmuring againft its
conqueror. But it muft not be forgotten that long before and long after
the War, as well as through its continuance, Wafhington was the object
of the envy and the calumny of others than the adherents of the
Englifh crown. The earlieft public outrage offered to his character
appears in the official *Mémoire*, fent in 1756 by Louis XV to the other
fovereigns of Europe, in which, referring to Wafhington's Ohio expedition and the death of Jumonville, in 1754, he fays : " Il parôit que l'im-
" pofture ne coûte rien à M. Wafinghton ; ici il f'en fait honneur." It
is amufing to find that Beaumarchais in 1779, replying to Gibbon's ftate-
ments and juftifying the aid given by France to America, heads his lift

of

of outrages exerciſed by England with this charge of aſſaſſination ! He did not know that the falſehood hit the chief of the Americans, inſtead of the Engliſh court. Perhaps the original aſſertion by a foe of this bald ſlander " may be forgiven, though it cannot be applauded :" but its repetition was unfortunate on the lips of a friend. But the friends of America in the war were not all friends of Waſhington. His appearance in uniform in the Congreſs of 1775, and the military ·experience he had acquired, undoubtedly familiarized the minds of ſome members with the idea of his nomination to be Commander of the Army : but the conſent of many of the delegates to this appointment was only extorted by the neceſſities of the caſe, and was a ſource "of real regret in nearly one half" of the gentlemen who made it. A number of the members were for Mr. Hancock ; more were for Charles Lee ; many for Waſhington ; but the greateſt number were in favour of Artemas Ward. There is room however for the inference that there was no deſire on the part of a majority to maintain at the continental expenſe a New England army, with New England officers, to fight New England battles on New England ſoil. There was a Southern party againſt a Northern ; " and ſo many of our " ſtaincheſt men," ſays Adams, " were in the plan, that we could carry " nothing without conceding to it. Another embaraſſment, which was " never publicly known, and which was carefully concealed by thoſe who " knew it, the Maſſachuſetts and other New England delegates were " divided. Mr. Hancock and Mr. Cuſhing hung back ; Mr. Paine did " not come forward, and even Mr. Samuel Adams was irreſolute. Mr. " Hancock himſelf had an ambition to be appointed Commander-in- " Chief * * * When I came to deſcribe Waſhington for the commander, " I never marked a more ſtriking and ſudden change of countenance. " Mortification and reſentment were expreſſed as forcibly as his (Han- " cock's) face could exhibit them." Mr. C. F. Adams adds that " neither " Hancock nor Ward was ever afterwards cordial towards " Waſhington. Nor were the Virginia delegates unanimous in his favour : " particularly " Mr. Pendleton was very clear and full againſt it." When the queſtion

was

23

.

was debated, there was a warm oppofition to Wafhington: on public, however, and not on any perfonal grounds. Pendleton, Sherman, Cufhing, and feveral others joined in it; fearing "difcontents in the army " and in New England." This army, it muft be recollected, confifted at that time almoft entirely of the men raifed by and in New England, and gathered before Bofton. There was in Congrefs a ftrong jealoufy of Maffachufetts, and a fufpicion of her real objects; and her reprefentatives were obliged to be very guarded in the expreffion of their fentiments, left other colonies fhould recoil from them. Wafhington's appointment, therefore, was juftly regarded by Adams as valuable, in fecuring the union of the colonies in defence of New England; and the troops forthwith raifed in the more fouthern provinces and fent thither by Congrefs juftified his predictions. And it muft likewife be remarked that at the time of the felection of Wafhington, Hancock writes favourably of the appointment. The pay of the General Officers was alfo a hard morfel for fome of the delegates to fwallow. Samuel and John Adams and Paine were earneft to reduce it, but in vain. "Thofe ideas of equality, which are fo agree-" able to us natives of *New-England*, are very difagreeable to many gen-" tlemen in the other Colonies. They had a great opinion of the high " importance of a Continental General, and were determined to place " him in an elevated point of light. They think the *Maffachufetts* " eftablifhment too high for the privates, and too low for the officers, and " they would have their own way." Probably the original fuggeftion of Wafhington for Commander-in-chief came from Johnfon of Maryland, or fome other Southern delegate; but to John Adams was due his public nomination. "Virginia is indebted to Maffachufetts for Wafhington," he boafted, "not Maffachufetts to Virginia. Maffachufetts made him a " general againft the inclination of Virginia." But this can only refer to the voice of the delegates from thefe States, who were generally intimately allied in Congrefs on any party queftion. Long after the Peace, John Jay faid that in the Congrefs of the Revolution there was always, from firft to laft, a moft bitter party againft Wafhington. What were the

various

various motives of its members, it is impoſſible to ſay, ſince their names even cannot, with fulneſs and accuracy, be now aſcertained. It is but fair, however, to give the benefit of a doubt, and to ſuppoſe that it was an apprehenſion of the effect which ſo much power and popularity might have on his ambition. The future was as yet unſeen; and many men knew not what would be the conſequences of the attainment of Independence. "The ſubjugation of my country," ſaid Edward Biddle, whoſe declining health had compelled him to forego the influence his talents would have given him as delegate in Congreſs from Pennſylvania—"I "deprecate as a moſt grievous calamity; and yet ſicken at the idea of "thirteen, unconnected, petty democracies: if we are to be independ-"ent, let us, in the name of *God*, at once have an empire, and place "*Waſhington* at the head of it." But this idea was not pleaſing to our people, whoſe experience of the benefits of monarchy was not great, and very few of whom had ever been diſtinguiſhed by any royal favour; or, as an Engliſh verſifier ſang:

> Poor loſt America, high honours miſſing,
> Knows nought of ſmile and nod, and ſweet hand-kiſſing:
> Knows nought of golden promiſes of kings;
> Knows nought of coronets, and ſtars, and ſtrings:
>   In ſolitude the lovely rebel ſighs!
> But vainly drops the penitential tear—
>   Deaf as the adder to the woman's cries,
> We ſuffer not her wail to wound our ear:
> For food, we bid her hopeleſs children prowl,
> And with the ſavage of the deſert howl.

But ſuch "fears of the brave and follies of the wiſe" are incident to human nature; and the jealouſy of Waſhington may have in ſome caſes been connected with honeſt though blind judgments. It was a public bleſſing, thought Adams, that the glorious defence of the Delaware forts, in 1777, was "not immediately due to the Commander-in-chief nor to "ſouthern

" fouthern troops. If it had been, idolatry and adulation would have
" been unbounded ; fo exceffive as to endanger our liberties, for what I
" know.   Now, we can allow a certain citizen to be wife, virtuous and
" good without thinking him a deity or a Saviour."   It was in the fame
year that the writer took fire in Congrefs at the fentiments entertained for
the General by certain members : " I am diftreffed to find fome of our
" members difpofed to idolize an image which their own hands have
" molten.   I fpeak of the fuperftitious veneration which is paid to General
" Wafhington.   I honour him for his good qualities, but in this houfe,
" I feel myfelf his fuperior.   In private life, I fhall always acknowledge
" him to be mine."   The *Cabal* againft Wafhington was never more
violent than at this time, and probably debate ran high and warm language was ufed on either fide : and his enemies, if we may rely on the
following anecdote, were more powerful in the Council-chamber than in
the Camp.   In a *Life of Lord Stirling* the father-in-law of William Duer,
written by Mr. Duer's fon (and the relationfhip is of fome importance to
the authenticity of the anecdote), occurs this fingular paffage : " It is
" related by Mr. Dunlap in his Hiftory of New York, upon the authority
" it is prefumed of the late General Morgan Lewis, that a day had been
" appointed by the *Cabal* in Congrefs for one of them to move for a
" Committee to proceed to the camp at Valley-Forge, to arreft General
" Wafhington; and that the motion would have fucceeded had they not
" unexpectedly loft the majority which they poffeffed when the meafure
" was determined on.   At that time, there were but two delegates in
" attendance from New York; Francis Lewis, the father of the late
" General Morgan Lewis, and William Duer, the fon-in-law of Lord
" Stirling—barely fufficient to entitle the State to a vote, if both were
" prefent.   But Mr. Duer was confined to his bed by a fevere and dan-
" gerous illnefs.   His colleague, Mr. Lewis, had fent an exprefs for Mr.
" Gouverneur Morris, one of the abfent members, who however had not
" arrived on the morning of the day on which the motion was to have
" been made.   Finding this to be the cafe, Mr. D. inquired of his phy-
                                                                " fician,

" ſician, Dr. John Jones, whether it was poſſible for him to be carried
" to the Court-Houſe where Congreſs ſat. The Doctor told him it was
" poſſible, but it would be at the riſk of his life. ' Do you mean,' ſaid
" Mr. D., ' that I ſhould expire before reaching the place?' ' No,' re-
" plied the Doctor, ' but I would not anſwer for your leaving it alive.'
" ' Very well, ſir,' ſaid Mr. D., ' you have done your duty, and I will
" do mine. Prepare a litter for me; if you will not, ſomebody elſe will—
" but I prefer your aid.' The litter was prepared, and the ſick man
" placed in it, when the arrival of Mr. Morris rendered the further uſe
" of it unneceſſary, and baffled the intrigue that had induced its prepara-
" tion." The date of this anecdote was ſuch as to render it extremely
improbable that the American Army, if it ſubmitted to Waſhington's
depoſal, would have ſtruck another blow under another leader for Congreſs. " I remember well," ſays a public writer in 1780, " that ſuch
" was the ſituation of the Army, while they lay at the Valley Forge in
" the winter of the year 1778, deſtitute of cloathing, many times in want
" of proviſions, and greatly diſcouraged, that a member of Congreſs, who
" had been on a Committee to the Camp to new model the troops with
" the advice of General Waſhington, declared to me, that ' ſuch had been
" the ſtate of things, that nothing but the great virtues of that man had
" kept the army together.' " Much concerning this *Cabal*, and its
workings in the Congreſs of 1778, exiſts in Gordon: whence it would
ſeem that delegates from Maſſachuſetts and Virginia were deep in the
affair. Samuel Adams, he ſays, was concerned in it, and adds: " The
" army was ſo confident of it, and ſo enraged, that perſons were ſtationed
" to watch him, as he approached the camp, on his return home. But
" he is commonly poſſeſſed of good intelligence, and was careful to keep
" at a ſafe diſtance. Had he fallen into the hands of the officers, when
" in that paroxiſm of reſentment, they would probably have handled him
" ſo as to have endangered his life, and tarniſhed their own honour."
There is a curious article in the *Pennſylvania Evening Poſt*, July 24th,
1779, which may refer to this anti-Waſhington Party in Congreſs: " a
" junto

" junto who have endeavored to fubject all things to themfelves, all power,
" civil military and marine: Who have endeavored to remove every
" perfon that would not mingle in their factious views; and to place none
" in office but their friends, relatives and dependents; againft whofe
" malevolence the unfullied fame of the great American patriot was but
" a flender barrier; whofe victim was a W********* — and whofe idol
" was a L**." The fame journal (July 9th, 1779) mentions the exiftence in Congrefs of a fort of Club of certain New England, New Jerfey,
and Pennfylvania delegates, with two or three from the Southward; the
foundation of which had been laid in the firft Congrefs, when there was
caufe to fear that New York and one or two other Middle Colonies were
averfe to extreme meafures. Among the Wafhington party in Congrefs,
I fhould put fuch names as thofe of Robert, Lewis, and Gouverneur
Morris; Jay; Paca; Burke; Drayton; Duane; Duer; Francis Lewis.
The queftion is not fo clear in regard to Samuel Adams; Mifflin; Wither-
fpoon; Rufh; Jefferfon; the Lees, &c.; though any conclufion to be
arrived at muft in fome meafure be conjectural. In 1789, Samuel Adams
in a manner denied to a friend the truth of Dr. Gordon's ftatement of his
having been concerned in a plot to remove Wafhington. And in 1796,
when John Adams was a fucceffful candidate for the Prefidency of the
United States, he makes an obfervation that would imply a well-eftablifhed
community of action between Samuel Adams and Thomas McKean:
" The feelings of friendfhip excite a curiofity to know how McKean will
" vote. By that I fhall guefs how Governor Adams would have voted."
On April 4th, 1778, Patrick Henry wrote to Richard Henry Lee that he
(Lee) was traduced in Virginia by perfons who alleged that he was engaged in a fcheme to difcard Wafhington: and in 1780, Dr. William
Shippen, jun. wrote thus to him of General Greene: " He is a little
" fufpicious that you are not perfectly fatiffied with his conduct, becaufe
" you were faid to be inimical to our commander, and of confequence
" to him, who was fuppofed to be one of his flatterers—this falfe
" idea I have reprobated to General Greene, and affured him he would
" find

" find you his friend and uſeful confidant." And it is ſaid alſo that the occaſion of Lee's loſing his popularity at home, and his ſeat in Congreſs in 1777, was chiefly becauſe he had compelled his tenants to pay their rents. His biographer and nameſake, in ſeveral places, flouts the charge made by Judge Johnſon, in the *Life of Greene*, that Richard Henry Lee was Waſhington's enemy. But if Samuel Adams was, ſo was, probably, Lee. It is at all events a gratifying thing to remark that no one, in later days, had the moral courage to confeſs that he was concerned in the buſi-neſs ; indeed its very name of *Conway's Cabal* ſhows that its members were afraid or aſhamed to avow their complicity ; for Conway was but a tool of the hour, whom it was eaſy enough for a fellow-ſoldier to ſilence, and whoſe name was affixed to a ſcheme (that he doubtleſs approved of, but which was concocted by longer heads than his own) merely to avert the attention of the world from its real authors. In the Army, indeed, the love and veneration for Waſhington was boundleſs, and almoſt univerſal ; and here truly lay the ſtumbling-block of his enemies. It was only in the immediate circle of ſome of the foreign-born officers, as Conway, Lee, and Gates, that an oppoſite opinion was heard. Lee's ſentiments in regard to " Waſhington and his puppies " are ſufficiently well known. " *Entre* " *nous* " he ſays to Gates in December, 1776, " a certain great man is " damnably deficient." " As to his talents for the command of an army," ſaid Gates to Graydon, ' with a French ſhrug,' " they were miſerable " indeed." The teſtimony of the civilian, who was forced to remove from a comfortable houſe in one place to a comfortable houſe in another, be-cauſe Waſhington, with vaſtly inferior forces could not drive Howe out of Philadelphia, would be amuſing but for the circumſtance that, himſelf in a poſition to obtain a comfortable dinner—" a good roaſt turkey, plain " pudding, and minced pies "—he could ſo grievouſly have miſconceived the condition of the Army in his vicinity. As Mr. William B. Reed juſtly obſerves, " the ſufferings of the Americans during their winter canton-" ment at the Valley Forge have been often deſcribed. They have never " been exaggerated." Yet in the end of December, 1777, after noticing

Howe's

Howe's movements, a Pennſylvania Whig remarks : " All this is done in
" the view of our Generals and our army, who are careleſs of us, but care-
" fully conſulting where they ſhall go to ſpend the winter in jollity, gaming
" and carouſing.   O tell not this in France or Spain !   Publiſh it not in
" the ſtreets of London, Liverpool or Briſtol, leſt the uncircumſiſed there
" ſhould rejoice, and ſhouting for joy, ſay " America is ours, for the
" rebels are diſmayed and afraid to fight us any longer !   O Americans,
" where is now your virtue ?   O Waſhington, where is your courage ?"
In this Nòte, no citation is made of Tory or Britiſh accuſations againſt
Waſhington.   One of theſe was, however, againſt his chaſtity : and ſome
of the charges went ſo far as to identify the woman and to trace the offſpring.
This is only recurred to here, becauſe of a like inſinuation being made
apparently by Charles Lee, to General Reed, in 1778; but with great propriety the latter repelled as unworthy of credence the ſlanders that charged
the Commander-in-chief with " great cruelty to his ſlaves in Virginia, and
" immorality of life, though they acknowledge it is ſo very ſecret that it
" is difficult to detect it."

In the cloſe of 1779, General Sullivan warned Waſhington that the
Cabal of 1777 againſt him ſtill exiſted, and waited only for ſufficient
ſtrength to attack him openly.   He therefore adviſes him to keep on his
guard.   " Appearances may deceive even an angel.   Could you have
" believed, four years ago, that thoſe adulators, thoſe perſons ſo tenderly
" and ſo friendly uſed, as were Gates, Mifflin, Reed, and Tudor, would
" become your ſecret and bitter, though unprovoked enemies.   If we view
" them now, we cannot help lamenting the want of ſincerity in mankind."

But everything ſaid or done during the War, by Whig or Tory, falls
far ſhort of the dreadful charges brought againſt Waſhington by his
political opponents and fellow-citizens in 1795, 1796, and 1797.   Compared with the language of *Valerius, Pittachus, A Calm Obſerver, &c.,*
former ſcurrility almoſt became praiſe.   Every variety of evil, from
avarice and fraud to tyranny and murder, was imputed to his hands,
with a power of conception and expreſſion that leaves us no room to
wonder.

wonder that he ſhould have diſdained to run the gauntlet of a third preſidential term ; that " he prudently retreated," to quote the remark of his
ſucceſſor. " Will not the world be led to conclude," ſays one, " that the
" maſk of political hypocriſy has been alike worn by a Cæſar, a Crom-
" well and a Waſhington !" " Had the meridian blaze of the Preſident's
" popularity continued much longer," writes another, " the lamp of
" American liberty would have been extinguiſhed forever. Happily for
" humanity, a change has taken place before it was too late, and the con-
" ſecrated ermine of preſidential Chaſtity ſeems too foul for time itſelf to
" bleach." In the *Philadelphia Aurora*, a paper edited with deteſtable
ability, will be found ſcores of pieces of a like nature. What can be
more lamentable than ſuch lines as theſe, publiſhed at the very epoch
(March 4th, 1797) of Waſhington's withdrawal to private life ? " 'Lord,
" letteſt now thy ſervant depart in peace, for mine eyes have ſeen thy
" ſalvation,' was the pious ejaculation of a man who beheld a flood of
" happineſs ruſhing in upon mankind. If ever there was a time, that
" would licenſe the reiteration of the exclamation, that time is now
" arrived : for the man who is the ſource of all the misfortunes of our
" country, is this day reduced to a level with his fellow-citizens, and is
" no longer poſſeſſed of a power to multiply evil upon the United States.
" If ever there was a period for rejoicing, this is the moment. Every
" heart in uniſon with the freedom and happineſs of the people, ought to
" beat high with exultation that the name of Waſhington from this day
" ceaſes to give a currency to political iniquity, and to legalize corrup-
" tion—a new æra is now opening upon us, an æra which promiſes much
" to the people ; for public meaſures muſt now ſtand upon their own
" merits, and nefarious projects can no longer be ſupported by a name.
" When a retroſpect is taken of the Waſhingtonian adminiſtration for eight
" years, it is a ſubject of the greateſt aſtoniſhment, that a ſingle individual
" ſhould have cankered the principles of republicaniſm in an enlightened
" people, juſt emerged from the gulf of deſpotiſm, and ſhould have carried
" his deſigns againſt public liberty ſo far, as to have put in jeopardy its

" very

" very exiftence : fuch, however, are the facts, and with thefe ftaring us
" in the face, this day ought to be a *jubilee* in the United States." In
1813, John Adams, writing to Jefferfon, refers to " the terrorifm excited
" by Genet, in 1793, when 10,000 people in the ftreets of Philadelphia,
" day after day, threatened to drag Wafhington out of his houfe, and
" effect a revolution in the government, or compel it to declare war in
" favor of the French revolution and againft England. The cooleft and
" the firmeft minds, even among the Quakers in Philadelphia, have given
" their opinions to me, that nothing but the yellow fever, which removed
" Dr. Hutchinfon and Jonathan Dickinfon Sergeant from this world,
" could have faved the United States from a fatal revolution of govern-
" ment." But Adams's morbid jealoufy of every one whofe fame out-
fhone or even (in his own opinion) rivalled his own, cankers very many of
his judgments on Wafhington. While Prefident himfelf, he complained
that he was annoyed by " puppets, danced upon the wires of two jugglers
" behind the fcenes ; and thefe jugglers were Hamilton and Wafhington."
In another and (as believed) unpublifhed manufcript, he fays (Aug. 23rd,
1806) : " The Federalifts, as they are called by themfelves and their
" enemies, have done themfelves and their country incalculable injury by
" making Wafhington their political, religious, and even moral pope, and
" afcribing every thing to him. Hancock, Samuel Adams, ———, and
" feveral others have been much more effential characters to America, than
" Wafhington. Another character, almoft forgotten, of more importance
" than any of them all, was James Otis. It is to offend againft Eternal
" juftice to give to one, as this people do, the merits of fo many. It is
" an effectual extinguifher of all patriotifm and all public virtue, and
" throws the nation entirely into the hands of intrigue. You lament the
" growth of corruption very juftly ; but there is none more poifonous
" than the eternal puffing and trumpetting of Wafhington and Franklin,
" and the inceffant abufe of the real Fathers of the country."

Defpite all that has been faid too of Mr. Jefferfon's relations with
Wafhington, it is difficult to hold that thefe really could have been of a
perfectly

perfectly ſincere and friendly nature. It was believed in Waſhington's family that ſhortly before his death he opened his mind very plainly to Mr. Jefferſon, in two or three letters. A gentleman, who was Waſhington's confidential clerk at the time, gives us ſome idea of their nature; for neither letters nor copies long continued in exiſtence after their writer was dead. "The firſt was," he ſaid, "rather a letter of inquiry; the ſecond one "was ſo ſevere, and excited his feelings ſo much, that the hair appeared "to riſe on his head as he recorded it, and he felt that it muſt produce a "duel—that the third was of a milder tone, but not a very gratifying "one."

It is not, at this day, too much to ſay, that the common ſuffrage of all that is wiſe and good in human nature, authorizes us to queſtion that man's ſoundneſs of judgment or rectitude of purpoſe, who impugns the character of *George Waſhington.*

INDEX.

LIST OF SUBSCRIBERS.

LARGE PAPER COPIES.

1 J. CARSON BREVOORT ;   Brooklyn.
2 JOHN CARTER BROWN ;   Providence.
3 JAMES LENOX ;   New York.
4 WILLIAM MENZIES ;   New York.
5 WINTHROP SARGENT ;   Natchez.

SMALL PAPER.

 1 S. ALOFSEN ;   Jerfey City.
 2 AMERICAN ANTIQUARIAN SOCIETY ;   Worcefter.
 3 ASTOR LIBRARY ;   New York.
 4 N. P. BAILEY ;   Kingfbridge, N. Y.
 5 GEORGE BANCROFT ;   New York.
 6 SAMUEL L. M. BARLOW ;   New York.
 7 J. R. BARTLETT ;   Providence.
 8 J. CARSON BREVOORT ;   New York.
 9 CHARLES I. BUSHNELL ;   New York.
10 WILLIAM ALLEN BUTLER ;   New York.
11 ERASTUS CORNING ;   Albany.
12 WILLIAM J. DAVIS ;   New York.
13 GILBERT C. DAVIDSON ;   Albany.
14 HENRY B. DAWSON ;   Morrifania.
15 SMITH ELY, JR. ;   New York.

16	John Fowler, Jr. ;	New York.
17	Eli French (3 copies) ;	New York.
20	Benjamin H. Hall ;	Troy.
21	William Howard Hart ;	Troy.
22	Z. Hosmer ;	Bofton.
23	Allan McLean Howard ;	Toronto.
24	Waldo Hutchins ;	New York.
25	James B. Kirker ;	New York.
26	George Law ;	New York.
27	Library Company ;	Philadelphia.
28	Benson J. Lossing ;	Poughkeepfie.
29	Henry S. McCall ;	Albany.
30	Maine Historical Society ;	Brunfwick.
31	William G. Medlicott ;	Longmeadow, Mafs.
32	William Menzies ;	New York.
33	Mercantile Library Association ;	New York.
34	Mercantile Library Society ;	Baltimore.
35	Military Academy ;	Weft Point.
36	Charles C. Moreau ;	New York.
37	John B. Moreau ;	New York.
38	T. Bailey Myers ;	Mofholu, N. Y.
39	New York State Library ;	Albany.
40	Henry Nicoll ;	New York.
41	Charles B. Norton (5 copies);	New York.
46	Ohio State Library ;	Columbus.
47	Richard H. Phelps ;	Windfor, Ct.
48	G. W. Pratt ;	New York.
49	J. V. L. Pruyn ;	Albany.
50	Joel Rathbone ;	Albany.
51	C. B. Richardson ;	New York.
52	George W. Riggs, Jr. ;	Wafhington.
53	John A. Russell ;	New York.
54	'Winthrop Sargent (5 copies) ;	Natchez.

64	DAVID SEARS ;	Boston.
65	J. GILMARY SHEA ;	New York.
66	HENRY A. SMITH ;	Cleveland.
67	W. B. SPRAGUE, JR. ;	Albany.
68	J. AUSTIN STEVENS ;	New York.
69	ROBERT TOWNSEND ;	Albany.
70	HOWARD TOWNSEND ;	Albany.
71	FRANKLIN TOWNSEND ;	Albany.
72	FREDERICK TOWNSEND ;	Albany.
73	W. B. TRASK ;	Boston.
74	WM. H. TUTHILL ;	Tipton, Iowa.
75	TOWNSEND WARD (10 copies) ;	Philadelphia.
85	WM. H. WHITEMAN ;	Philadelphia.
86	W. H. WHITMORE ;	Boston.
87	H. AUSTIN WHITNEY ;	Boston.
88	WM. A. YOUNG ;	Albany.